DISPLAY

REA

3 1833 03616 0213

P9-DTL-053

The BLACKWELL BROTHERS

From Bachelors to Bridegrooms!

Sara's sweetness was drawing him deeper and deeper....

And for the first time in his life, Cutter felt powerless to control something.

Sara's gentle ways and tender nature were in sharp contrast to the harsh, cynical world he'd lived in most of his life. And her innocence seemed like a balm, easing his aching soul.

And Cutter realized he wasn't thinking about his mission, about his target. He was thinking about Sara.

He couldn't deny that he wanted to touch Sara Gunter, to taste the sweetness of her lips. But it wasn't just her body he wanted to touch. That would have been too simple.

This yearning, this need, went far deeper. He wanted to touch Sara's untouched heart and her fragile, sheltered soul.

And Cutter suddenly realized...

ROMANCE

He was on very dangerous ground.

Dear Reader,

With spring just around the corner, Silhouette's yearlong 20th Anniversary celebration marches on as we continue to bring you the best and brightest stars and the most compelling stories ever in Special Edition!

Top author Sherryl Woods kicks off the month with *Dylan and the Baby Doctor,* a riveting secret baby story in the next installment of AND BABY MAKES THREE: THE DELACOURTS OF TEXAS.

From beloved author Marie Ferrarella, you'll love *Found: His Perfect Wife,* an emotional story in which a man loses his memory and gains a temporary spouse.... And reader favorite Victoria Pade continues her popular cowboy series A RANCHING FAMILY with *Cowboy's Caress,* a heartwarming story about a woman who's ready to travel the world—until love comes to town!

Millionaire's Instant Baby is rising star Allison Leigh's must-read contribution to the series SO MANY BABIES. In this provocative story, a dashing tycoon gets more than he bargained for when he hires a single mom as his pretend wife in order to close a business deal.

THE BLACKWELL BROTHERS continue to capture hearts in the next book of Sharon De Vita's cross-line series. In *The Marriage Promise,* a Blackwell brother is determined to woo and win the forbidden love of a beautiful Amish virgin. And you won't want to miss *Good Morning, Stranger,* Laurie Campbell's dramatically poignant story about a woman, a child and a handsome, mysterious stranger who uncover secrets that bring together a meant-to-be family.

It's a month chock-full of great reading and terrific variety, and we hope you enjoy all the stories!

All the best,
Karen Taylor Richman
Senior Editor

Please address questions and book requests to:
Silhouette Reader Service
U.S.: 3010 Walden Ave., P.O. Box 1325, Buffalo, NY 14269
Canadian: P.O. Box 609, Fort Erie, Ont. L2A 5X3

SHARON
DE VITA

THE MARRIAGE PROMISE

Published by Silhouette Books
America's Publisher of Contemporary Romance

If you purchased this book without a cover you should be aware that this book is stolen property. It was reported as "unsold and destroyed" to the publisher, and neither the author nor the publisher has received any payment for this "stripped book."

This book is dedicated to Two Wise Men:
Edward M. Boss
Dr. Scott De Valk
With thanks and appreciation for your help,
your wisdom and your faith in my son.
May you always be blessed.

 SILHOUETTE BOOKS

ISBN 0-373-24313-8

THE MARRIAGE PROMISE

Copyright © 2000 by Sharon De Vita

All rights reserved. Except for use in any review, the reproduction or utilization of this work in whole or in part in any form by any electronic, mechanical or other means, now known or hereafter invented, including xerography, photocopying and recording, or in any information storage or retrieval system, is forbidden without the written permission of the editorial office, Silhouette Books, 300 East 42nd Street, New York, NY 10017 U.S.A.

All characters in this book have no existence outside the imagination of the author and have no relation whatsoever to anyone bearing the same name or names. They are not even distantly inspired by any individual known or unknown to the author, and all incidents are pure invention.

This edition published by arrangement with Harlequin Books S.A.

® and TM are trademarks of Harlequin Books S.A., used under license. Trademarks indicated with ® are registered in the United States Patent and Trademark Office, the Canadian Trade Marks Office and in other countries.

Visit us at www.romance.net

Printed in U.S.A.

Books by Sharon De Vita

SHARON DE VITA

is a *USA Today* bestselling, award-winning author of numerous works of fiction and nonfiction. Her first novel won a national writing competition for Best Unpublished Romance Novel of 1985. This award-winning book, *Heavenly Match,* was subsequently published by Silhouette in 1986.

A frequent guest speaker and lecturer at conferences and seminars across the country, Sharon is currently an Adjunct Professor of Literature and Communications at a private college in the Midwest. With over one million copies of her novels in print, Sharon's professional credentials have earned her a place in *Who's Who in American Authors, Editors and Poets* as well as the *International Who's Who of Authors*. In 1987, Sharon was the proud recipient of *Romantic Times Magazine*'s Lifetime Achievement Award for Excellence in Writing.

IT'S OUR 20th ANNIVERSARY!
We'll be celebrating all year, continuing with these fabulous titles, on sale in March 2000.

Special Edition

#1309 Dylan and the Baby Doctor
Sherryl Woods

#1310 Found: His Perfect Wife
Marie Ferrarella

#1311 Cowboy's Caress
Victoria Pade

#1312 Millionaire's Instant Baby
Allison Leigh

#1313 The Marriage Promise
Sharon De Vita

#1314 Good Morning, Stranger
Laurie Campbell

Intimate Moments

#991 Get Lucky
Suzanne Brockmann

#992 A Ranching Man
Linda Turner

#993 Just a Wedding Away
Monica McLean

#994 Accidental Father
Lauren Nichols

#995 Saving Grace
RaeAnne Thayne

#996 The Long Hot Summer
Wendy Rosnau

Romance

#1432 A Royal Masquerade
Arlene James

#1433 Oh, Babies!
Susan Meier

#1434 Just the Man She Needed
Karen Rose Smith

#1435 The Baby Magnet
Terry Essig

#1436 Callie, Get Your Groom
Julianna Morris

#1437 What the Cowboy Prescribes...
Mary Starleigh

Desire

#1279 A Cowboy's Secret
Anne McAllister

#1280 The Doctor Wore Spurs
Leanne Banks

#1281 A Whole Lot of Love
Justine Davis

#1282 The Earl Takes a Bride
Kathryn Jensen

#1283 The Pregnant Virgin
Anne Eames

#1284 Marriage for Sale
Carol Devine

Prologue

He woke up in a bed with clean sheets and a real pillow. Blinking in fear and confusion, he rubbed his eyes, then sat up, brushing the tangle of dark hair off his eyes.

"So you're awake."

Cutter froze, then warily glared at the woman sitting in the chair next to the bed. Fists clenched, he narrowed his gaze on her as recognition seeped through him.

Her.

The mark—the one he'd snatched the purse from.

Weak-kneed, and with his belly aching from hunger, he'd spotted her, and the next thing he knew he was racing down the alley, clutching the big purse like a lifeline.

The last thing he remembered was leaning against the brick wall in the alley, trying to catch his breath and stop the world from spinning as he counted out the cash in her wallet.

Then everything went black.

He stared at her, his empty stomach now jumping in fear. She looked like an angel, dressed all in white, with soft hair and smiling eyes.

"Where am I?" He tried to sound tough, but his voice cracked and came out trembling. Terror-stricken, he glanced around. Sunlight was streaming in through the open window, and a slight breeze ruffled the dainty white curtains. He glared at her. "And who the hell are you?"

"My name is Emma. Emma Blackwell." She smiled. "And you're home, son." Emma rose, then came to stand next to the bed, a tender smile on her face.

"Home?" He snorted in disgust. "This ain't my home." He shoved off the sheet and tried to get up. Still wobbly, he simply couldn't manage it. He fell back against the pillows, furious at himself. "I ain't got no home," he snarled, fighting back tears of fear and frustration. "I don't belong nowhere to no one. Never have. Never will." Hadn't that been drilled into his head by his pa as long as he could remember?

"That's not true," Emma said gently, sitting at the foot of the bed. "You belong here, with us."

He glanced around suspiciously, refusing to hope. From somewhere in another part of the house he could hear a dog yelping and kids whooping. The smell of food was drifting through the air, making his stomach growl and his head ache, reminding him how long it had been since his belly was full.

"Who's us?" he asked warily.

"My husband, Justin, our housekeeper, Sadie, and our two boys, Hunter and Colt. You saw them that day in town."

He frowned. "You mean yesterday."

"No," Emma said with a smile. "That was two days ago."

"Jeez. I been here two days?" He didn't remember anything except the deep, dark blackness that seemed to suck him in. Another thought crowded his mind. "Where's the dough? The three hundred bucks?" The three hundred he'd snatched out of her purse.

She reached for a small, dainty handkerchief lying on the night table. It had a thin satin ribbon in a pretty shade of pink wrapped around it.

"Right here." She handed him the handkerchief. It carried the faint scent of her perfume. "You can keep it." She smiled. "And you'll find that the Blackwells always keep their promises."

Ignoring the sissy pink ribbon, he clutched the

handkerchief tightly in his fist, wondering what her game was.

Defiant, he glared at her, wishing his chin wasn't trembling. "Why'd you bring me here?"

"Well, I thought you could use some food and some rest." She chewed her lower lip as if contemplating a sudden thought. "I was thinking. Why don't you just stick around for a few days, just until you're feeling stronger?" Her smile made him feel as if someone had turned on the sun. "Hunter and Colt would love to have someone to play baseball with." She laughed, a soft, musical laugh that sounded like angels. Or at least what he thought angels would sound like.

He'd known too much misery in ten short years to believe in goodness. But from somewhere deep inside, a flicker of hope, small and greedy, began to glow.

He wondered how it would feel to be able to sleep in a bedroom like this, with clean sheets that didn't smell of booze, and a fresh breeze that brushed like silk against his heated, bruised skin.

And food, glorious, wonderful food. Hopefully enough to keep the awful stomach pains away. His stomach flipped, and he let his eyes slide shut, trying not to hope, to want, to yearn.

"We'd really like you to stay, son."

Son.

The word reverberated in his mind. Nobody had

3 1833 03616 0213

ever wanted him as their son, especially not the poor excuse for a father who'd set him out on the streets to steal for him, then beat him when he came home empty-handed.

Disgusted, he'd lit out of there, figuring he'd do better on his own. And he hadn't stopped running until he ran smack-dab into an angel with a soft voice and a gentle, caring smile.

"Son," Emma said gently, reaching out to gently brush a damp tangle of black hair off his still-bruised face, "do you think you might tell me your name?"

He swallowed hard, warily watching her eyes and her hands, ready to bolt if she lifted a hand to him.

"Cut-Cutter," he stammered. Her touch was gentle as she stroked his hair. No one had ever touched him with kindness before.

"Cutter." Emma kept stroking his hair. "Well, Cutter, why don't you stay? At least until you're feeling stronger."

"I can leave whenever I want?" Suspicious, he stared at her, eyes narrowed in challenge.

"Whenever you want," Emma confirmed.

"And I can keep the money?" He clutched the hankie tighter. If he had dough, he had freedom to flee anytime he wanted. Money always meant freedom.

"Every penny of it for as long as you want."

"Why?"

"Because I want you to believe that you can trust

me. I want you to know that the Blackwells keep their word." She took a breath. "And, Cutter, I want you to know that everyone belongs somewhere to someone." Her gaze, calm, steady and loving, met his. "And I want you to know that I believe destiny brought you to us. This is where you belong."

It had taken Emma almost six months to allay his suspicions, and another six to make him believe, but by then, it was too late. She'd worked her motherly magic.

Cutter had become a part of their family: a Blackwell, just like their other adopted boys, Hunter and Colt.

Over the years, Cutter grew to trust his adoptive father, Justin, with a fierceness that stemmed from deep within his soul. From Justin, Cutter learned about honor, integrity, and especially about what it took to be a man. What Justin taught him had nothing to do with fists or strength, but character and love.

Colt and Hunter taught him about brothers and the precious relationship and loyalty they shared. Like the three musketeers, the Blackwell boys stuck together. If someone picked on one, he'd have to take them all on. They had been three lost, lonely little boys, united not by blood, but by memories of childhoods gone bad. All three of them, Hunter, Colt and Cutter, had been granted a miracle: two people who'd taken a chance and given them a home, and a family, along with a fierce, protective love that had no beginning and no end. But over the years it was his adoptive mother, Emma, who taught Cutter about the power and the miracle of love. Even though he never completely lost his suspicion of people, even though he carried the battle scars of his youth etched in his heart as a reminder of what trusting the wrong people could do, Cutter hesitantly, reluctantly, finally learned to love.

His family.

His brothers, his father and especially his mother.

Still, just in case, Cutter Blackwell always carried that wadded-up handkerchief full of money with him. *Just in case.*

Chapter One

Twenty-five years later

Cutter Blackwell never expected to find another angel. He figured a guy was only entitled to one miracle in his life.

But the moment he laid eyes on Sara Gunter, Cutter felt something hard and cold shift and soften in his scarred, suspicious heart.

It scared the hell out of him.

It had taken him nearly six months to find her, and after so many years in the military, he knew better than to walk into a situation before he'd had a chance to familiarize himself with the terrain of an operation.

He was nothing if not cautious and observant, weighing every angle, assessing any danger, making sure he knew every escape route, every exit, before making his move. Which was why, for the third day in a row, he was leaning against a towering old oak along a barren road in a small Amish community in southern Illinois.

Watching an angel.

When his mother Emma first asked him to try to find Sara, a woman he suspected was his brother Colt's natural sister—a sister Colt never even knew about—he'd spent months doing research. He'd treated her request just like a hundred other covert military operations he'd been involved in during the past twelve years before his retirement. Cutter had been surprised to learn she'd been adopted as a toddler into an Amish family.

He knew better than to make the situation personal. Letting his emotions get involved in a mission had almost gotten him and three of his best men killed.

He'd vowed then never to make the same mistake.

He couldn't think about the fact that he was on this mission purely as a favor for his mother, or to reunite his older brother with a long-lost sister. Cutter knew he had to treat it with the same cold, calm indifference that had kept him alive for so many years as he traveled from one hot spot in the world to another, doing the kind of work people lied about and died for.

The woman he'd been searching for wasn't a person to him—merely the target. It was just another way to ensure success and familiarize himself with the situation.

Now, with Sara in view and the rough bark of the oak tree cutting into his back, Cutter shifted his weight, dragging a hand through his rakishly long black hair, allowing his gaze to follow Sara and the little boy who always seemed to be with her.

Thoughtfully, he watched them. He knew the boy was her brother Josef, six, and also adopted.

Cutter's gaze shifted to Sara and he studied her with the casual disinterest a scientist would study a specimen under a microscope, trying to ignore the sudden emotions that had erupted as if from some long slumber.

Tilting his head, he couldn't hear what she was saying to the child, but he banked a smile as he watched her gently scold the boy.

A faint evening breeze ruffled the ribbons of Sara's white prayer *kapp,* the *kapp* that covered nearly all her glorious raven hair. Hair, he thought with a scowl, that was nearly the identical shade as his brother Colt's, reinforcing his belief that he'd finally found the right target.

Even dressed in traditional Amish garb—a long-sleeved dark dress that nearly covered her from stem to stern, dark stockings and a stiff, starched dark apron—there was no denying the hint of Sara's womanly curves beneath the styleless outfit.

She reminded him of a storybook princess, all peaches and cream and sweet, gentle innocence—an innocence he'd forgotten still existed.

He'd learned Sara was a teacher—actually the only teacher in the one-room Amish school in their community. And although most of the Amish were reluctant to discuss one of their own with a stranger, he'd been fortunate to have a contact who knew Sara.

Luckily, the military, at least the covert part he'd once been involved in, was like one big family. Harlen "Endy" Enderly, a retired operative, who lived near the settlement had welcomed him, not exactly with open arms, but he'd allowed him to stay in his home once he realized that Cutter was on the level.

Cutter explained that he had no wish or intention to hurt or bring harm to Sara Gunter. His only mission was to inform Sara of her real family—her brother, a sibling she never even knew existed.

So for the past few days, since he'd arrived in town, he and Endy had swapped stories about their occasionally illustrious pasts while Cutter had quietly watched Sara and waited for the right opportunity to make his presence known.

He'd been patient and observant, but he was a man who instinctively knew the time to make his move.

And the time was now.

Stepping back deeper into the late-afternoon shadows, Cutter continued to study Sara as he absently fingered the wadded-up, nearly threadbare handkerchief full of money that he'd literally carried with him through hell and high water ever since he was a child.

It was his own version of a security blanket, he figured as he watched Sara pause along the road to say something to the child.

With a sigh, Cutter turned and headed back toward Endy's house, wanting to reach it before Sara did. Destiny had seen fit to push him into the path of another angel, he thought with a weary, worried sigh.

And Cutter Blackwell was a man who'd been taught at an early age to believe in destiny. He might not trust it, but his mother, another angel, had taught him to believe in it.

He turned and glanced at Sara one last, long, lingering time, wondering what it was about *this* angel that had suddenly snared his undivided attention.

"Do I have to go home, Sara? Can I walk with you along the road for a while longer, Sara?"

Swinging the straw basket that hung from her arm, Sara Gunter smiled at her six-year-old brother as he limped along beside her. "Do you not have chores to do this afternoon, Josef?"

He grinned, lifting his good leg and kicking another pebble with the toe of his black shoe before awkwardly balancing himself to bend and pick it up.

"I have chores," he said with a grin that revealed two missing teeth as he examined the pebble. He tipped his hatted blond head back to watch the pebble as he sent it flying through the air. "But I also have time to walk with you."

The child picked up another pebble and was about to send it flying when Sara reached out her free hand to stop him. "Do not toss pebbles, Josef. You could hit something, an animal or bird, perhaps."

The child's eyes widened in alarm and his chin trembled for a moment before he glanced into the distance where the first pebble had landed harmlessly. "I did not think, Sara." Tears filled his eyes, then dripped down his rosy, freckled cheeks. "Do you think I hurt something?"

"No, Josef, I do not think you have hurt anything." Smiling, she gave his wide-brimmed black hat an affectionate tug. "But it is always better to be safe than to be reckless."

"Reckless." He repeated the foreign word, his brows drawing tightly together as they started walking again. Mindful of his damaged foot, Sara slowed her pace so he could keep up with her. "Sara, what is this…'reckless'?" he asked, still frowning.

In spite of the fact that both she and her brother had been adopted, they were incredibly alike in many ways, one of which was their inherent curiosity. It both delighted and alarmed her. On many occasions her strict father had chastised her, for it was not their way to be curious, to thirst for worldly knowledge or for more than what was provided to them by God and their faith.

"Reckless." Sara ran her tongue over her teeth, trying to think of how to explain the word to him. "Reckless, Josef, means to do something...dangerous."

"Dangerous," the little boy repeated slowly, giving it some thought.

"Yes. To do or say something that might hurt you or someone or something else."

His steps paused on the dry gravel road as he glanced up at her. "And was I...reckless?" Josef asked. "By throwing a pebble? Did I hurt someone or something, Sara?"

His crestfallen face tugged at her heart. "Not this time, Josef," she said softly, laying a tender hand on his shoulder. "But you must take care never to harm anything or anyone, not even unintentionally—not on purpose," she immediately amended, seeing the confusion in his eyes at her use of a word he didn't understand.

"I will not be reckless again, Sara," he said solemnly. "Not even un...un...unintentionally. I will promise."

She smiled her approval. "Good, Josef. Very good."

He slipped his hand in hers as they began walking again. "Are you going to see Mr. Enderly today?"

Sara's smile was huge and genuine. "Yes, Josef, you know I go there every Friday after class to care for him."

"And will you stay the weekend?"

"Yes, Josef. This is an off Sunday. We do not have services, so I will stay until it's time for school again on Monday morning to care for Mr. Enderly." She frowned, glancing in the direction of the elderly gentleman's house. "You know he has not been well lately."

"I know, Sara," Josef said soberly, then he grinned. "And will you look at his big fat books today?"

"Josef!" Sara came to an abrupt halt. "Have you been spying on me?"

"Spying?" The boy thought for a moment, then grinned impishly. "No, not spying, Sara, but when I walked with you the last time, I peeked in the window and saw a room with all those books." His grin widened. "I know how you like books."

"It is not good to be peeking, Josef." She tried to make her voice stern but failed miserably. The love she felt for her baby brother was immeasurable.

"I know, Sara," he said, taking her hand again. "But so many books I have never seen before." He glanced up at her. "What did they say?"

Sara laughed. "I do not know, Josef. And you should not be asking so many questions."

To no one would she admit that one of the joys of working for Mr. Enderly was being able to sneak a peek now and then at his books.

They were like magic to her, filled with wisdom

and knowledge, knowledge that she longed for, knowledge that was not a part of her world. For as long as she could remember, she had had this desire to learn. To see. To discover. And she suffered the guilt of it.

Home and family were the heart of the Amish way and the most important part of their faith. They had no need for English book learning when all they needed to know they could learn from the Good Book.

Sara glanced at Josef, wondering if perhaps her father had been correct when he accused her of influencing her brother and putting fancy English ideas of book learning in his head.

"Josef, I think you should go home now. Mama will be worried if you don't come straight home from school." She straightened his hat. "You're later than usual since you stayed to help me clean up today."

She smiled. On Fridays she always cleaned up her schoolroom so it would be ready for her and the children on Monday. And Josef always stayed to help.

"Do I have to, Sara?" He glanced down the road. "We're almost to Mr. Enderly's and I was hoping to look at the room of books again."

Smiling, she tugged his hat again, feeling her heart ache for him. "Not today, Josef. But I promise one day soon I will ask Mr. Enderly to let you see the book room." She took a step closer to him, tipping his chin up to meet his eyes. "But, Josef, you must never, ever tell about this need to see the room of books.'' There was a hushed sense of urgency in her voice, not just for herself, but for him. ''Do you understand me?''

''But why?'' He blinked up at her, looking confused. His face sobered, and his eyes filled with fear. ''Is it...against the *Ordnung* to want to see the books?'' he whispered, terrified at doing something forbidden.

The *Ordnung* were the rules that governed their *Gemeide*—their church district—and ultimately their lives. Rules that were not meant to isolate, but to protect the family, for family was of the utmost importance.

At six, Josef was technically not bound by the rules of the *Ordnung*—at least not until he was baptized— when he became an adult. Children were allowed to wait until they were adults before making a choice about devoting their lives to God.

Once Josef was an adult and ready to marry, he would make his choice. If he chose to continue in this way of life, then he'd be baptized and his life would forever be governed by the *Ordnung* of their settlement.

Just as hers would be in just a few short months, Sara thought, trying not to frown.

Her father had been hinting that he wanted her to go riding with Joshua, her neighbor and oldest, and dearest, childhood friend. Such a serious matter, go-

ing riding with a man, would indicate to the settlement the man's intentions.

And Sara knew that her father and Joshua believed
she would make Joshua a good wife. Unfortunately,
Sara wasn't so certain she was ready to make a life-
long commitment to Joshua—or to the settlement.

With a sigh, Sara brushed back an errant strand of
hair, knowing that all too soon, ready or not, she
would have to make a decision. A momentous decision that could forever change her life. Until then, she
was not technically bound by the *Ordnung*.

Not that she would ever do anything to defy the
settlement's rules. She knew no other way to live, and
in spite of the fact that at times she chafed under the
constraints of their *Ordnung*, she knew that ultimately
it was for the good of the people.

Or so she'd been told for as long as she could remember. It wasn't that she doubted it, no, it was just
that she wasn't certain she was…ready. But how
could she explain rules she also wasn't certain she
entirely understood to a six-year-old? Carefully, she
decided with a smile, putting all her teacher's skills
to work.

"Josef," she began slowly, "you know that it is
not good to want more than what God has provided.
To want more is to be…ungrateful, and that is a sin.
Do you understand?"

"Sara?" Josef's face was clouded with confusion.
"I do not understand something. If God gave us all

that we have and need, then did he not give Mr. Enderly his room of books, too?''

Out of the mouths of babes, Sara thought with an inward sigh, wondering how to answer her brother.

They had been taught and believed that everything they had God had provided. Everything that happened was God's will and they were not to question or defy God's plans, so how could she explain that God had provided the books, but to want to learn from them was wrong?

She couldn't, she realized sadly, especially since she had never understood it herself. So how did she expect a six-year-old to understand?

She didn't, so Sara decided the best answer for now was no answer.

''Run along now, Josef, and I will see you at school on Monday.'' She reached into her supper basket and pulled out a chocolate chip cookie she had made last night. ''Here, something for the walk home.''

Greedily, he eyed the cookie before snatching it from her hand and taking a big bite. ''Good day to you, Sara,'' he said around a mouthful of cookie.

''Good day to you, Josef,'' she said with a smile and a wave. ''Go straight home so you won't worry Mama.''

''I will.'' Walking backward slowly, he waved as he shoved the rest of the cookie into his mouth.

She watched him for a moment before turning to continue on her way, trying to contain her own excitement. Her sensible black shoes made no sound on the dry gravel; her steps were measured and careful, but inside, ahh, inside Sara's fertile mind her shoes were…dancing.

It was hard to contain her excitement. Such excitement had been with her from the day she had accepted the job with Endy, caring for him and his home.

And especially his room of books.

Working for Endy was not really a job, but an…adventure. An adventure that always made her smile and awakened the pesky longings she'd tried to keep buried deep within her curious heart.

Even though their neighbor was *anna Satt Leit,* an outsider, not one of the people, her father had permitted her to accept the position as the money she earned helped provide for the family and the farm. Since they were such a small family, her father did not have the many hands of sons others had to help out, so extra money was always welcome.

Caring for another, particularly one who was elderly and ailing and had no family or children of his own did not go against the *Ordnung.*

Even though Endy was English, he had lived on the outskirts of their settlement for many years and had proven to be a good neighbor, and more importantly, a good man. A man the deacons and church elders had come to admire and accept in spite of the fact that he was not one of them. Endy respected their beliefs, traditions and their ways, even if they were not his ways.

With a sigh, Sara swung the basket higher and turned down the road that led to Endy's house. She loved this time of year when spring was just waiting to burst free and the days grew longer and the air smelled of newness and possibilities.

She thought of Endy again and how grateful she was for his friendship. Spending time with him, in his house, gave her a glimpse of life outside the settlement. And she treasured every single moment.

They would share the supper she'd prepared last night and then she would sit wide-eyed, mesmerized, listening to Endy's stories of the places he'd been, the things he'd seen, the people he'd known. His adventures.

To no one would she admit that she longed for such things. Longed to see something more than the rolling acres and meandering fields that surrounded her home, where two-story farmhouses, stables and poultry coops dotted the landscape.

She glanced around with a sigh of longing. She yearned to experience something other than life in the settlement, longed to meet and speak with others who had lived different lives.

Forbidden lives, she thought, instantly feeling a rush of guilt.

She should not be yearning for things that were impossible. Forbidden to her. It was sinful, she knew;

instead, she should be appreciating the life God had provided for her.

But no matter how much guilt ate at her, she could not stop the longing in her heart to learn, to be able to sit and pour over the magical words and knowledge within the leather-bound books in Endy's study until her eyes blurred from all the reading.

Oh, to have such a thrill, such an adventure, to be free to learn all that she was curious about was more than she could ever hope for or imagine.

Sara shook her head, sending the ribbons of her prayer *kapp* swaying, trying to banish the heavy burden that troubled her conscience and her heart.

Swinging the supper basket to her other arm, Sara sighed as she climbed the steep, paved driveway that led to Endy's small two-story, wood-framed home.

The sun was lying low in the sky as she lifted a hand to knock on the door. As the door opened, she looked up with a smile that froze on her lips.

"Hello, Sara," a stranger said.

Chapter Two

Mesmerized, Sara's mouth fell open at the man filling the doorway. Unconsciously, she took a step back, but for some odd reason she wasn't afraid.

Surprised, but not afraid.

He was a stranger in that she had never met him, and yet something, somewhere deep in her woman's heart, recognized him as one would recognize someone they had known a lifetime.

Stunned, she could only stare at him, eyes wide, heart thundering, while the basket slid unheeded from her arm.

"I'm sorry," he said, catching the basket midair. "I didn't mean to scare you."

Still staring and starting to tremble, Sara blinked up at the man. The two of them stood immobile, staring wordlessly at one another for long moments.

"Who...who are you?" Sara finally asked.

Very few English ever came to their settlement. It was disturbing to see a stranger here. Sara swallowed hard, trying to find her voice, wondering how he knew her, unable to drag her gaze from his.

Trembling in earnest now, she made herself look around him. "Where...where is Endy?"

"Right here, Sara honey." Endy pushed open the screen door with a smile, and she heaved a relieved sigh. "I've been waiting for you. Come on in. I want you to meet someone."

Eying the stranger warily, Sara slipped past him carefully, so as not to touch him. Her long skirt rustled against the leg of his pants as she passed, and Sara felt a thrumming response in return, a response at such intimacy that stunned her.

Once inside, she clasped her now empty hands in front of her, unbearably nervous and not knowing what had brought on such foreign feelings.

"Sara honey, I want you to meet my nephew, Cutter Blackwell."

"Your nephew?" Sara repeated softly, her startled gaze darting from Endy to Cutter. Her eyes flashed for a moment as her chin lifted. "You mean the no-account who cares so little for his family he stays away for many years and does not bother to worry about your care?''

"Yep, that's me." Cutter said, grinning. "The no-account nephew. But my absence couldn't be helped," Cutter explained by way of apology, exchanging a quick glance with Endy. "I've been...out of the country.''

"Cutter's been in the military, honey. Defending his country. That's why it's taken him so long to look me up."

"I see," Sara said, clearly seeing nothing of the kind. She wondered what kind of country put fighting above family. The English world was odd indeed.

She looked at Cutter even though his dark, fathomless eyes made her stomach feel as if a flock of frantic butterflies had settled there.

Lacing her fingers together, Sara rocked back on her sturdy black heels and lifted her chin. "Fighting is as good a reason as any, I suppose, to ignore your family." The hint of censure in her voice and the flash in her eyes made both men exchange a glance and a smile.

"Now don't be too hard on the boy," Endy cajoled. "I understand Cutter's absence, honey. I spent many a year in the military myself and I can attest there is no finer calling."

Based on her words and her actions, Sara realized belatedly that the man—both men—would think she had no manners. Ach, what was wrong with her today? she wondered. Spring foolishness again.

"I am truly sorry." Shyly, she glanced at the unbearably handsome stranger and then quickly at Endy, for looking at the English man did something wicked to her pulse. "I did not mean to embarrass you or to judge."

Other than Endy, she'd never actually met an English man. But she'd wondered relentlessly, letting her mind wander to all the possibilities of what English men were like. They had always seemed so foreign, so dangerous, so...exciting to her. And none more so than the man who now stood before her, dressed in his fine English clothes, with his dark stubbled chin and rakish black hair. He was unlike any man she'd ever met.

No wonder she was nervous coming face-to-face with him, especially since he seemed to know her even if she didn't know him.

Sara struggled to regain her composure, lacing her fingers more tightly together. "I am ashamed for my behavior. I did not mean to make you feel unwelcome." She lowered her gaze again. "It is not for me to judge," she repeated softly.

"No apology is necessary, Sara," Cutter said.

Watching her carefully, he realized he was not accustomed to having someone, especially a woman, look at her shoes when she spoke to him and it bothered him.

Without thinking, he slowly, gently, lifted her chin so their eyes met. The moment he touched her, he felt something quick, hot and unbearably tender wrap around his guarded heart.

He'd never felt so vulnerable, so naked, or so utterly defenseless in all his life, and he was a man who had never been defenseless.

About anything.

Ever.

Until this moment when he looked into the face of another angel.

Her eyes, so blue, so wide, met his and he felt it again, that flash of heated, intense emotions that made him react as if he'd taken a sucker punch to the gut. Or been blindsided by a sniper in the dark of night.

Narrowing his gaze, Cutter tried to put things in perspective. To use all the skills and resources he'd learned in his training to remain objective.

Never get emotionally involved with a target.

It was one of the first lessons he'd learned in the military. One he'd only forgotten once before, and then it had nearly killed him. He couldn't afford to forget that lesson ever again.

Trying to remain detached and trying to inject some perspective into the situation, Cutter studied Sara.

There was a smudge of fatigue under her eyes, and he realized something was worrying sweet Sara. What, he wondered, was it that put those shadows under her eyes? What did she think about in the middle of the night, when she lay in her bed all alone, staring into the darkness?

As he thought about Sara all alone in her bed, he rubbed his thumb across her chin and felt the hot arc of awareness all the way to his toes.

Her skin was softer than the finest silk, her eyes as blue as cornflowers. He drew in a slow, shaky breath as his gaze met, then clung to hers. Standing there looking into Sara's eyes, he saw all the goodness he'd once long ago stopped believing in.

It scared him as nothing had in a long time.

He watched as Sara's hand fluttered to her heart and her mouth opened into a soft O. Her reaction made Cutter smile, and all the suspicion and caution he'd carried with him like baggage since his youth seemed to slip away for a moment.

He was certain he'd never met anyone quite so innocent or quite so wary in his life. From her reaction, Sara obviously wasn't accustomed to having a man touch her. He could see the shock and then the fleeting moment when desire flitted through her eyes. He wondered if she even realized what it was.

Probably not, he decided, wondering why the thought pleased him so much.

"I'm sorry," he said softly, unable to resist rubbing his thumb across the tender skin beneath her chin again, enchanted by its feel.

He heard the distant warning echoing loudly in his mind and let his hand drop to his side. Careful, he cautioned himself. He was treading on very dangerous ground here and he couldn't afford to get distracted. Unconsciously, Cutter rubbed a finger against his thumb and swore he could still feel the warmth of her.

He watched her glance at her shoes, then swallow hard as she hesitantly raised her gaze to meet his. Her eyes were so blue he felt as if he could get lost in them. At the same time, it was unnerving that looking into her eyes was like looking into his brother Colt's.

Even though her hair was pulled back and almost completely covered by the bonnet she wore, a few wisps had slipped free and now framed her delicate face. He could see her hair was the same rich, glossy ebony as Colt's.

His brother Colt. No, he corrected. *Her brother Colt.*

It was just the reality check he needed to put things back into perspective, he thought, emotionally withdrawing from the situation.

He couldn't allow himself to get involved with a target. It was too dangerous. Too risky. And in this instance, far too personal.

However, the look on her face aroused all his protective instincts. Instincts he never realized he had.

But then he'd always been a sucker for the unprotected, maybe because he knew what it was like. He'd never forgotten the nightmare of his youth, before

Justin and Emma Blackwell had rescued him and given him a reason to hope, to love.

It wasn't their fault he'd never learned to trust anyone but his family.

Watching Sara, feeling what he was feeling, Cutter knew he'd have to move very, very carefully with her. From the innocence in her eyes, he knew she'd trust too easily, and with this mission he'd undertaken, he knew he couldn't afford to let her trust him.

It wouldn't be fair because he had to deceive her in order to successfully achieve his objective. It was one of the perils of the job. But he would try to do nothing to harm or frighten her, nor would he do anything to cause her to fear him.

It was a promise he intended to keep.

"Come along, now, Sara," Endy said. "I've been waiting all day for one of your wonderful home-cooked meals." Endy took the basket from Cutter and headed into the small kitchen. "I told Cutter all about your fine home cooking," he said over his shoulder.

"I don't want to impose," Cutter said.

"Oh, no, please." Horrified that she had made the man feel unwelcome in his own uncle's home, Sara rushed to make amends. "It would be an honor to welcome and serve you at our table."

She finally smiled, pressing her clasped hands to her tummy to stop its trembling. She'd been stunned by his casual touch earlier. Men did not touch casually in her life. It was only within the sanctity of marriage, blessed by God and the church, that a man could freely touch a woman.

But this man had touched her freely, as if they had known each other forever, and not only for a few brief moments.

And Sara realized with some surprise that she liked the gentle touch of this man.

"I have prepared plenty, more than enough for everyone, so please, come join us."

Sara walked into the small kitchen where Endy had already begun setting the table and Cutter followed her.

"Sit. This is my job," Sara told Endy with a laugh, taking a plate from him and setting it down as she began pulling covered bowls and dishes out of the large basket she had brought with her, grateful to have something to do with her trembling hands. "Have you had a long journey?" Sara asked Cutter as he pulled out a chair and sat, watching her.

"Pretty far," he admitted. "I came up from Texas."

Her eyes widened for an instant, then she nodded in understanding. "Then you must be tired and hungry from your long journey."

She set a large bowl on the table and removed the cover to reveal perfectly cooked beef swimming in carrots, celery and onions on the table.

"It only took about two and a half hours to make

the trip,'' he said, causing Sara to stop what she was doing to stare at him.

Suddenly, she shook her head and laughed, making the black wisps of curls framing her face dance. ''You must have a very speedy horse and buggy to come all that way in just over two hours.'' The sound of her laughter drifted merrily through the quiet room. ''Such a fine animal I must see.''

Cutter laughed. ''I didn't ride. I flew. On an airplane,'' he clarified.

''I see.'' For an instant, Sara stared dreamily into space, feeling a well of longing so strong she had to resist the urge to sit right down and ask him all about his flying adventure.

What would it be like, she wondered, to climb into a machine that could fly into the sky like a bird, taking you higher than the clouds and across miles and miles? A smile drifted across her face. Such a thing must be incredible.

Knowing such longings were futile, Sara turned from the table to get the fresh milk she'd brought.

''And how long will you be with us?'' she asked as she stood on tiptoe to get three clean glasses from the cupboard.

''I'm not sure how long,'' Cutter said. ''Maybe a week or so.''

Sara set the glasses on the table and tried not to smile. A week. For some foolish reason, the thought of having him around for that long made her feel a warm, inexplicable happiness. Perhaps during that week he might share some of his adventures or tell her of the places he'd been and the things he'd done.

She was being foolish, she realized, just as her father had always scolded. She knew she shouldn't be daydreaming about Cutter Blackwell when there were so many more serious things for her to do. Mentally, she gave herself a shake.

Cutter was a fine-looking English man and had no use for or interest in an Amish woman who knew nothing of his ways or his world and wanted to ply him only with questions to satisfy her curiosity.

He would no doubt have many English women to entertain with his tales. Why would he even want to bother with her?

The unspoken thoughts were like a bucket of ice water, momentarily dousing her curiosity, her longings, as well as her happiness.

Stealing a glance at him, Sara sighed, knowing the yearnings she'd held deep inside her were futile.

Her life, her destiny, were already laid out for her, and, looking at Cutter Blackwell, for the first time since she was a child, she didn't feel shame or even embarrassment, but simply deep, sincere regret.

Chapter Three

"So how's Josef?" Endy asked, helping himself to some stew as Sara poured fresh milk into their glasses, setting them at each place.

Determined to be pleasant in spite of her own inner turmoil, Sara broke into a beautiful, beaming smile at the mention of her brother.

"He is fine, Endy. Thank you for asking."

"Josef is Sara's little brother," Endy explained to Cutter. "What is he now, Sara? About six?"

"Yes." Smoothing her dress and apron down, Sara took her place at the table, then bowed her head in silent prayer.

Respectful of her customs, Cutter and Endy did the

same, listening quietly as Sara's soft, musical voice whispered a blessing in German.

When she looked up, Cutter was watching her and she flushed again. "I have asked for God's blessing," she explained with a smile. "For this wonderful food he has bestowed on us."

Cutter nodded but said nothing, taking the bowl of stew Endy passed to him.

"So you have a little brother," Cutter prompted.

"Yes, Josef is a wonderful boy. Always helpful and kind." Love echoed in Sara's voice.

"Do you have a big family?" Cutter asked.

Sara dared a glance at him and felt that queer fluttering in her stomach once again. Cutter Blackwell was a fine-looking man, she decided. Perhaps that was why she felt so...odd every time she looked at him.

"No," she replied, a hint of sadness in her voice. She pushed the food around her plate. "We are a very small family for Amish. Unfortunately..." She paused. "My brother and I, we...we...were both...adopted."

Sara shifted uncomfortably and lowered her gaze to her plate. "Adopted" was an English word, not really part of their life. She knew that her parents had not gone through any legal formalities since the people didn't recognize such laws or regulations. All she knew was that neither she nor her brother had been born to their mother.

"Is there a problem with being adopted in your community?"

"Problem?" She considered that for a moment. "No, not a problem, I don't think. Home and children are considered the true worth of an Amish family," she continued. "Children are a family's strength, their sole purpose for being." She did not want to explain to this English man the circumstances of how she came to be the Gunters only daughter. She couldn't even if she wanted to because she simply didn't know.

"So the smaller the family, the less worth?" Cutter asked.

"In a way," she replied hesitantly, embarrassed to discuss such a personal matter with a stranger who had no knowledge of their ways. "It is always a joy to the settlement to be blessed with many children."

Sara sighed. Her mother's barrenness had served as a black mark against the entire family. Although not ostracized, they were, nevertheless, not as highly regarded as some of the others in their *Gemeide* simply because of their small family.

Sara had often wondered if perhaps that was why her father had always been so strict, so rigid, as if he could garner the respect of his peers—the elders and the deacons—by being overly pious in his devotion.

"So you and your brother were both adopted, huh?"

"Yes," she said with a nod, passing Cutter a platter

of roast potatoes, hoping to change the subject. This was not something she'd ever discussed with anyone.

Watching her, Cutter had no idea how a woman like her, so innocent, so fragile, would cope with the knowledge of who he really was and why he was here.

Or how he'd made his living.

She was a woman who lived in a totally different environment. She lived a life unlike any he'd ever imagined or thought possible, and he had to admit, for once in his life, he was thrown for a loop.

As he watched Sara, he felt guilty all of a sudden. Telling her the truth about himself would force her to face something she might not want to face.

And he wasn't entirely certain he had the right to do such a thing to her.

He had learned firsthand how important family was; had learned it first by not having one and then by having the Blackwell's take him into their home and into their hearts, making him part of their family.

He wondered if it was fair to thrust Sara, innocent Sara, into a hornet's nest—learning she had two families. Her real family, Colt and the parents she'd been taken away from when she was just a baby. And her adoptive family, the Gunters, who had raised her in a world that was as foreign to him as his was to her.

Somehow the stakes seemed to have risen, and Cutter knew he'd have to tread carefully.

For all their sakes.

Aware that he was sitting there staring at her, Sara tried hide to keep the turmoil she was feeling. But she'd had no experience with this sort of thing. No experience feeling flustered and breathless in the company of a stranger.

A male stranger, and an English man at that, one who kept looking at her as if he had a million questions and she the only one with answers.

Taking a bite of her food, Sara swallowed, then glanced up at him. "And what of the rest of your family, Cutter Blackwell?" She liked the way his name sounded on her tongue. It was simple and easy to say and seemed to fit him. "Do you have family other than your uncle?" She glanced at Endy affectionately.

Cutter hesitated for a moment, wondering exactly how truthful to be. "I was adopted, too," he said slowly, helping himself to more stew. He had to admit she was an excellent cook.

"Adopted?"

Sara's eyes widened in delight. It was clearly not the answer she had been expecting. She had never met anyone else who had been adopted before, other than her brother Josef. Such a thing was a rarity in their community.

Sara glanced down at her plate, pushing a bit of beef around with her fork. To no one would she ever, ever admit that she had long been curious about her birth family. It was hard not to wonder who she really was, where she'd come from and whom she'd been born to.

Hard, too, to wonder why her birth mother had given her away. It brought an unexpected pain to her tender heart whenever she thought of it, but her curiosity was such that once, when she was small and not so good at controlling or concealing her innate curiosity, she had asked her mama about her birth family, about how she had come to live with the Gunters.

She'd only inquired once.

Big, silent tears had shaken her mother's shoulders, and she'd clutched Sara tightly to her ample breasts, rocking her back and forth as sobs shook her body.

It had frightened Sara as nothing else had before or since. She'd never really seen her mother cry before, certainly not like that. In that moment, she'd vowed never again to do or say anything to cause her mother pain or to cry like that.

And she never had.

But she never forgot her questions or lost her curiosity. But as with everything else in her life that seemed foreign and forbidden, she kept her questions and her curiosity buried close to her heart where no one could see.

Smiling, she set her fork down, unexpectedly pleased to know that she and Cutter had something in common. It immediately set off a round of questions in her mind, questions that seemed to just pop right out of her mouth.

"And do you have a big family, Cutter Blackwell?"

"Not so big, I guess," he admitted with a shrug. "I have two brothers."

"Brothers." She laughed, shaking her head. So they had something else in common. "Brothers can be a handful. Especially younger brothers. And what are your brothers' names? Are they older or younger?"

Cutter laughed at her exuberance, leaning back in his chair to watch her. "I have one younger brother. His name is Hunter and he's a Lipan Apache. He's also the town pediatrician."

Sara's brows drew together. "What is this Lipan Apache?"

Not for the first time did she wish she'd been able to study more, to gain access to all the knowledge that had always seemed to beckon to her. Knowledge her father and the deacons had deemed unnecessary for any Amish woman who had no need to know of anything but what their mothers and the Good Book taught.

"Lipans are a tribe of Native American Indians. Hunter is only one of about a hundred actual Lipan Apaches still living," Cutter said, smiling. "Hunter just got married a few months ago."

"Married." With a dreamy sigh, Sara rested her

chin on her hand, wondering what it would be like to fall in love and marry.

Wonderful, she decided. And very romantic. In their settlement, as in most Amish settlements, a mate was generally chosen by a woman's father, chosen not because of love, but because of a potential partner's skills as a farmer and father.

She let out another sigh, then realized with a start that Cutter was staring at her again.

She straightened and picked up her fork. "And what does your brother do as a…a pediatrician?" she asked, bringing her mind back to the conversation and savoring the new word.

"Hunter's a doctor, a children's specialist," he said.

Sara frowned thoughtfully. "And your brother, he can fix…hurt children?"

She thought of her brother Josef, of the limp that was with him every day. It made her sad to know that her brother would carry such a burden for his whole life.

When Josef had first come to them and begun walking, his limp had been very visible. Always curious, she had asked her parents why they could not take Josef to the doctor in town to have his leg fixed. She'd been told that Josef's limp was God's will. The people believed everything happened for a reason. And they would do nothing to go against the will of God.

She didn't truly understand then, nor did she understand now how God could give a little boy such an affliction. An affliction that made even simple things difficult for him.

It pained her to watch little Josef struggle to do things other little boys took for granted, like climbing into the wagon or scrambling up the haystack. But he had never once complained; he'd accepted his handicap the way children everywhere accept any part of their life as normal.

God's will, Sara thought again, struggling to understand and not question.

"Yes," Cutter said. "My brother Hunter spends most of his time helping hurt or sick children."

"I see," Sara said. "And so what of your other brother? Who is he and what does he do?"

Nerves were part of any mission, but for the first time in his life, Cutter had to force himself to control his now, as he thought about his brother Colt and his own reason for being here.

"Colt's the oldest of us boys," he said carefully. He glanced at her, aware that Colt's name hadn't seemed to register with her.

He didn't know if he felt relief.

Or regret.

He wanted to tell her the truth when the time was right and in his own way. But for that, he would need some time to learn more about Sara, time to learn more about her situation, time to assess exactly how to go about telling her the truth so that the information would disrupt her life as little as possible.

The last thing he wanted to do was hurt her.

Or his brother Colt, who was just as innocent as Sara in this regard.

Cutter again chose his words with care. "Colt's the sheriff of our town, Blackwell, Texas."

"A sheriff?" Sara said, her eyes wide. "You mean your brother Colt is a real cowboy?"

Cutter laughed at how delighted that news made her. "Yes, I guess you could say he's a real cowboy."

"Imagine that," Endy chimed in with a chuckle, before pushing his plate away. He coughed, then cleared his throat, causing both Sara and Cutter to look at him with some concern. "If you two'll excuse me, I think I'm going to go rest a bit." He patted his tummy. "I think I ate too fast."

Sara was on her feet instantly, her face creased in worry. "Endy, is there something I can do?" She hurried around the table toward him. "Would you like me to warm some milk? It always makes your stomach feel better."

Endy smiled, then stifled a yawn. "No, not just now. You two go on with dinner and your conversation." Endy got to his feet. "Sit, sit, Sara honey," he said, waiting until she reluctantly did. "I'll just go up and rest." He smiled at her frown. "Don't fret, Sara, please. I'm sure I'll be fine in no time. I have a doctor's appointment tomorrow, and I'll just mention this little episode to him." Endy glanced at Cutter. "Still think you'll be able to drive me into town tomorrow afternoon to see the doc?"

"Sure thing," Cutter said, leaning back in his chair.

Endy turned to Sara. "If you don't mind, honey, would you keep Cutter here company for me tonight?" Endy rubbed his stomach again. "I hate leaving him all alone. Well, I think I'd best call it a night."

"Of course, Endy, of course." Sara flushed at her own eagerness, feeling guilty for so looking forward to the prospect of spending more time with Cutter Blackwell. She frowned suddenly. "Are you sure you're all right, though?"

Endy smiled, leaning over to pat her hand. "Don't worry, hon, I'm fine. I think it's just a case of good old-fashioned indigestion." Endy pushed his chair in, then glanced at Cutter, shaking his head. "Your brother's a cowboy. Imagine that."

Laughing, Endy shook his head harder as he headed out of the kitchen.

Sara watched him with a worried expression for a long moment, then slowly turned toward Cutter, her face suffusing with heat when she realized that they were suddenly, inexplicably…alone.

Chapter Four

Not certain whether Endy was trying to give him some leeway here and time alone with Sara, or if the man was truly feeling ill, Cutter didn't want to add to his guilt by having Sara upset by Endy's condition. Watching concern shadow her features, Cutter decided to shift her attention back to their conversation.

"Sara?"

She'd dropped her gaze, but now she lifted it to him, trying to curb the tingle that was singing along her every nerve ending.

She forced a smile, trying to put her worry for Endy and her fear of being alone with Cutter aside. She'd already embarrassed herself once this evening; she wouldn't do it again. She was an adult, and Endy had asked her to play hostess to his nephew.

She was doing nothing wrong, she told herself. Merely doing a favor for an ill friend.

"So Cutter Blackwell, your brother Colt…is he really a cowboy?"

"Yep."

Sara leaned forward, her excitement over his announcement overshadowing her concern for her friend. "And does he wear a shiny badge? And boots? Real cowboy boots?"

"Yep," Cutter admitted with a laugh, wondering how Colt would feel if he ever heard him describing him like some Saturday morning cartoon character. He'd probably deck him. "Colt does indeed wear a shiny badge and a big hat." He grinned. "A Stetson."

"A Stetson?" she repeated with a frown, savoring the new word. "What is this Stetson?"

He smiled. "It's the kind of hat he wears."

"Oh, my!" Sara's eyes gleamed with wonder. "I cannot wait to tell my brother Josef."

She laughed excitedly. The sound was light, carefree and slid easily along Cutter's nerve endings making them sit up and take notice.

"Josef is utterly fascinated with the idea of cowboys and badges. He will be thrilled to know that I have actually spoken to the brother of a real cowboy from Texas, one who wears a badge."

"That's definitely my brother." Your brother, too, Cutter added silently.

"And boots?" she prompted, not wanting to miss a single detail, knowing it would delight Josef. "Does your cowboy sheriff brother actually wear boots?"

Cutter chuckled. "Definitely boots, Sara. Colt is rarely without his boots."

Still resting her hand on her chin, Sara stared at him, mesmerized by what he had told her. Compared to her own, his life and family seemed full of adventure and excitement.

"And is your brother Colt married, as well?"

Cutter shook his head, hooking his arm over the back of his chair. "Colt, married?" The thought made him smile. "I don't think Colt will ever settle down." His smile widened. "At least not with one woman when there are so many in the world."

"Oh." Some of the joy in her eyes dimmed and she pressed a hand to her mouth. "Does your brother Colt not wish to have a family or be happy?"

In her world, a man who was not married, who did not have a family, could never truly be fulfilled. All men were meant to mate. It was God's destiny for a man to take a wife, to have a family.

Cutter was thoughtful for a moment, wondering how the heck he could explain his footloose and fancy-free flirt of a brother, or the fact that the idea of getting married was about the equivalent of being buried alive in his brother Colt's book.

He had a feeling this was not something sweet Sara would readily understand.

Deliberately, he softened his answer. "I just don't think Colt has found the right woman yet." His answer made her smile. "When he does, he'll probably settle down and get married and have a family."

About the same time that chickens wear dentures and dancing shoes.

Other than family, Colt didn't form attachments to people, especially not to women.

Nor did Cutter.

Especially not to a particular woman.

At least he and Colt had that in common.

"You have a very interesting family, Cutter Blackwell."

"We've been called a lot of things, Sara, but interesting has never been one of them."

"And your brothers, are they adopted, as well?" she asked, unable to believe she was asking these questions of a stranger. But the curiosity about him and his adoptive family seemed to burn in her heart.

"Yes. Hunter was the first of us to be adopted. He was abandoned on my parents' front porch when he was about five or six."

"Abandoned?" Sara's gaze searched his for a moment as she wondered if perhaps she had misunderstood. She was unable to imagine anyone abandoning their own child. A child was God's blessing, a precious miracle to be savored, to be loved—their purpose for living.

Not for the first time did she wonder about her own mother—her natural mother.

It still hurt, Sara realized sadly. Deeply.

In her own way, she, too, had been abandoned, she reflected. At least by her birth family. And once again she wondered what had been wrong with her to cause her own mother, her own father, not to want her.

Sara shook the thought away, unwilling and unable to dwell on it. She had to appreciate the family who had taken her in and loved her, provided for her and made a home for her.

She had to accept it as God's will. He gave suffering to make each of them stronger, and she had to learn that this pain she'd carried around her whole life was meant for some purpose. To make her stronger, of course, to teach her to endure and perhaps not question what God had destined for her.

She had to learn to stop yearning for what she did not have, but to appreciate all that God had given her and accept her destiny as He decreed.

Unfortunately, she'd always had a hard time doing that.

"And what of your brother Colt?" Sara asked, forcing a tentative smile that didn't quite reach her eyes. "Was he, too, adopted?"

Watching her, Cutter realized he'd touched a nerve. He saw now that he'd have to be more cautious with his words. Adoption and abandonment were obviously sore subjects with her.

Instinctively, he understood as only one who'd experienced being abandoned and adopted could. Stalling, Cutter blew out a breath, choosing his words carefully.

"Colt, well, Colt was the second of us to be adopted." Unconsciously, his fists clenched, and he glanced away. What he was about to tell her was not just Colt's family history, but her own, as well.

"One Christmas Eve, when Colt was about eight or nine, his mother went out and left him and his baby brother alone in their apartment. There was a fire. Even though Colt was finally rescued by a neighbor, he almost died trying to save his kid brother."

Cutter rubbed his hands across his face, trying to wipe away the gut-wrenching sorrow he always felt whenever he thought about Colt's life before the Blackwell's had rescued him.

They'd all had it rough, but neither he nor Hunter had had it as bad as Colt.

"Mein Godt!" Tears swam in Sara's eyes. "I am so sorry for you." She swallowed, and her eyes shut against such horror, a horror she could not even begin to imagine. "And I am so sorry for your brother."

Instinctively, she lifted a hand and covered Cutter's, wanting to comfort him, to ease the pain she saw in his face, his eyes. Comforting came naturally to her; her nurturing instincts had always run strong, and not just for family, but for her students, for everyone.

At her touch, Cutter's hands clenched and he struggled to contain his emotions.

Not just my brother, he thought, *but your brother, as well.*

His eyes grew wary, hooded, as his gaze drifted to Sara's hand covering his. The only other woman who had ever touched him in comfort was his mother, Emma.

Oh, he'd had women over the years. They'd touched his body, of course, in pleasure, in lust, but never in comfort.

It seemed so...intimate it totally unnerved him.

Unaccustomed to the warmth and vulnerability Sara's touch evoked, it took all his courage not to pull away from her.

What the hell was wrong with him? Cutter wondered in disgust. He couldn't jeopardize a mission just because of his own sappy emotions.

He had to get a grip.

"The state took custody of Colt on the spot. It turned out the volunteer fireman who rescued him was Justin Blackwell. Colt spent a couple of weeks in the hospital recuperating, then the Child Welfare Agency arranged for the Blackwell's to have custody of Colt, and eventually they adopted him."

Sara's tear-filled eyes searched his. "And his

brother?'' she whispered. ''What happened to his baby brother?''

Cutter shook his head. ''He, uh, didn't make it.''

Cutter knew Colt had never forgiven himself for it. Colt had blamed himself for his brother's death and let guilt, grief and remorse eat him alive. Which probably explained why Colt didn't ''do'' Christmas. Ever. Christmas came and Colt went. Anywhere. Everywhere. Alone.

It was the only thing their parents had never been able to help Colt with, not that they'd ever given up trying.

''I'm so sorry, Cutter Blackwell,'' Sara said, swallowing past the lump in her throat. From the pain in Cutter's voice, she knew that his brother Colt's pain was one he shared. He obviously loved his adopted brothers deeply. This, too, she understood. ''I understand what it feels like to love a brother very much,'' she said softly, wiping her eyes. ''I love Josef very much, as well. I could not bear it if anything ever happened to him.'' She patted his hand. ''You and your brothers must be very close.''

''Yeah, we're all pretty tight.'' At her confused look, he explained with a smile, ''Close. We're a close family.'' He'd have to remember to watch his language, especially the slang. She obviously wasn't accustomed to hearing it. Nor did she understand it.

Curious, Sara looked at him. ''And what about you,

Cutter Blackwell? How did you come to be adopted by the Blackwells?''

She wondered where her brazenness had come from. But somehow Cutter did not make her feel ashamed or uncomfortable for asking. It pleased her.

He sighed, aware that he was growing accustomed to having her hand, warm and soft, over his. He realized he just might like the idea of Sara comforting him. Too much. It worried him.

He tried to stifle a grin. ''I, uh, made the mistake of trying to steal my mother's purse.''

Sara's eyes widened and she looked horrified. ''You stole from your mother?'' Her voice edged upward in shock, making his grin widen.

''Well, she wasn't my mother at the time. Just another mark,'' he added softly, unwilling, unable to tell Sara anymore.

She'd never understand the life he'd lived, what he'd done to survive. Such ugliness had no place in sweet Sara's innocent life.

''Mark?'' Sara's brows rose. ''What an unusual name for your mother.''

Cutter couldn't help laughing. ''No,'' he said, shaking his head. ''My mother's name isn't Mark. It's Emma. Emma Blackwell.''

''Emma?'' She frowned, not understanding why he would call his mother Mark if her name was Emma. Perhaps it was another odd English custom. ''What happened when you tried to steal the purse?''

"I passed out cold at Emma Blackwell's feet," he admitted, chuckling.

She smiled, pleased. "So you were not such a good thief, then?"

"No, actually..." He changed his mind, not wanting to admit the truth. "I was a terrible thief." It wasn't really a lie. He'd been a terrible thief. At least that day. "The next thing I knew I was tucked into a clean, warm bed in the Blackwell house." He shrugged, suddenly feeling humbled and a bit embarrassed by his confession. "I never left."

"The Blackwells adopted you then, as well?"

"Yeah." He blew out a breath. "That they did."

"And does this mean, Cutter Blackwell, that I should hide my purse from you?"

Her teasing surprised him and he laughed. "No, Sara. I've given up mugging and purse snatching for other pursuits."

She beamed at him, pleased that he'd had a happy life. "It seems to me, Cutter Blackwell, that you and your brothers are very fortunate. You have a wonderful family."

He smiled. "That we do, Sara. That we do."

Sara's eyes gleamed with wonder. Such a beautiful smile, she thought, watching him. It made his eyes light up and his face soften. Cutter was a very handsome, interesting man and she was enjoying their conversation. Sara continued to stare at him, her curiosity filling her head, making her dizzy.

She wondered why he'd tried to steal Emma Blackwell's purse and why he'd passed out at her feet.

More importantly, Sara wondered what had happened to his real family.

His birth family.

No matter how deep her curiosity, she could not bring herself to ask him. Some things were too personal, too private and occasionally too painful to talk about. Perhaps this was why Cutter Blackwell didn't care to discuss his birth family.

For her, never knowing about her birth family or why they had abandoned her had always been like a rusty knife in her heart.

Banishing her thoughts, Sara picked up the platter of food. "Would you like some more beef?" she asked politely, swallowing the questions that crowded on her tongue, trying to remember to be a good hostess.

"No." Cutter pushed his plate away and rubbed his stomach. "I'm full. You're a wonderful cook, Sara." His gaze sought hers and she wondered why such a compliment from this man made her feel almost giddy.

But it did, and she felt the giddiness flee as guilt took over.

What she felt, pleased by his compliment, was *Hochmut.* Pride. A sin. Ach, what on earth was wrong with her today? She was behaving in a way that was not suitable.

She'd treated this man like a stranger in his uncle's house, made him feel unwelcome and then asked him a million questions to make him think she had no manners.

And to top it off, she had been staring at him as if she had not ever seen a man before. English or not, he was still just a man, and she knew better than to behave in a manner that could bring embarrassment to her family and her friends.

She should not be pleased by this man's sweet words, nor should she be curious about his life or adventures. He was not part of her life, nor should she wonder about his.

Unable to prevent herself, Sara glanced at Cutter again, her gaze slowly going over his features. He was, she decided, a most attractive, interesting man. So very different from the men in the settlement.

Perhaps that was why she found herself so curious, she reasoned. His face was bare, and she had to admit she found it incredibly attractive. Almost all the men in the settlement wore beards, at least the married ones.

Cutter's face was deeply chiseled and his features were striking. His dark, mysterious eyes seemed to capture and hold her attention, making her want to stare into them as if they held the secrets of the world. Just looking at him made her heart pound and her pulse skid.

The feelings Cutter Blackwell aroused in her frightened her as nothing had in a long, long while.

With a sharp tinge of regret, Sara realized that there was no place in her life for a man like him.

And no place in his for a woman like her.

It was, she realized sadly, God's will. And no amount of yearning would change it.

Immediately, Sara rose, guilt propelling her to her feet. "Thank you, Cutter Blackwell, for enjoying the meal and for sharing your family with me."

She began clearing the table, needing to do something to take her mind off her thoughts.

"I will take care to clean up the kitchen quickly, so you can enjoy the evening."

The less time she spent with this handsome English man the better. She did not like the way she responded to him. He made her want to ask questions, and more importantly, seek answers, something she had spent most of her life trying to quell.

She made the mistake of glancing at him one last time and found her gaze caught by his. Her breathing seemed to slow as something strange and foreign unfurled inside her.

A moment ticked by. Then two…three…

Realizing they were alone and just staring at each other, Sara flushed, deliberately turned from him, then busily got to work.

She hurried through her task, feeling unnerved.

Perhaps it was best if she stayed out of Cutter's way while he was visiting his uncle.

She felt odd and unbalanced in his presence, and although she found him fine-looking and interesting and longed to ask him more questions about his life and adventures, as well as his adoption, she dared not. He frightened her on a level she had not known existed. Frightened her because when he looked at her, her heart seemed to speed up and her legs grew weak.

She found herself wanting to look at him, to let her gaze seek his, to let her eyes trace the fine, broad features of his face—his cheeks, his jawline, his mouth.

His mouth.

Her gaze seemed drawn to it, and she tilted her head, lost in her own thoughts, her own feelings. She had watched that mouth smile and laugh, and she wondered now what it would feel like to have that mouth touch hers.

Like the gentle caress of a butterfly's wing.

"Sara?"

She almost dropped the platter she was holding as her face flamed and her gaze lifted to his once again. She could see the amusement in his eyes and felt her flush deepen.

It would not do to go on daydreaming and spinning unrealistic romantic fantasies about an English man. Such a thing was foolhardy and could only lead to trouble. She knew better; had been taught better.

"Let me help." Cutter rose to his feet, lifting his plate to clear it from the table, but Sara rushed forward.

"Ach, please, no." She shook her head. "This is woman's work. I will do it."

He laughed. "Don't let Sadie hear you say that. She had us clearing the table ever since we could reach it."

Sara's heart slowed a bit, and she averted her gaze from his, unable to look at him. "And this Sadie, she is your wife?" she asked quietly, wondering why the thought brought such a sharp ache.

Why had she not realized that he would have a wife? A fine-looking English man with gentle hands and a sweet smile would of course have a wife to love and care for him. Perhaps children to warm his heart.

Slowly, shyly, unable to resist, she lifted her gaze to his and felt her heart thud recklessly within her breast. He had such beautiful eyes. So dark, so mysterious, and yet there was kindness in their depths, and gentleness.

It was unusual to see such kindness in a man's eyes. Her father and most of the men of their community were stern and stoic, rarely smiling in pleasure or laughing in joy.

Somehow she had a feeling Cutter Blackwell smiled in pleasure and laughed in joy.

For an instant, she longed to hear it; to hear the

sound of his laughter fill her house. To see his smile brighten her life. But there was sadness there, too, she realized. A sadness she couldn't help but recognize.

What had caused such sadness? she wondered. Then she was instantly brought up short when she remembered, she should not be wondering such things about any man, but especially a *married* English man.

Feeling foolish, Sara reached for the plate, but Cutter held on.

"Sara, Sadie is not my wife. I'm not married. Never been married." For some reason, it seemed very important to make it clear to her that he had no wife.

Yes, it might be important to the mission, but right now he was more concerned with making sure Sara knew that he was free.

If he'd stopped to ponder that thought, he might have cautioned himself not to get emotionally involved, but he didn't. His gaze searched hers and Sara felt her knees go weak again.

"Sadie is the Blackwell family housekeeper," he explained to her startled face. "She's been with us since my mom and dad were married. She's like part of the family and runs the house and especially the kitchen with an iron fist."

Sara absorbed his words in welcome relief, her knees almost sagging.

He had no wife.

Why the thought pleased her she could not say; Sara only knew that it did. Tremendously.

She frowned suddenly, trying to understand his words. "What is this...this iron fist your Sadie uses to run her home?"

Cutter laughed. "Sadie doesn't really have an iron fist," he said, not wanting her to get the wrong idea. "It's just an expression."

"An expression?" she repeated. "But what does this 'iron fist' expression mean?"

Rubbing his brow, he tried to think of how to explain it to her. "It just means that Sadie's very strict about her kitchen and whom she allows in it. My brothers and I were always trying to sneak in and steal a cookie while she was baking."

"Ach, now I understand," Sara said with a nod and a smile. "It is hard to run a kitchen with three brothers running around in it." She laughed. "Or even one brother intent on making mischief."

She made the mistake of looking up into his eyes and saw that kindness in them again. It seemed to call to her.

He was standing so close, with only the plate separating them. His nearness made her palms dampen and she feared she'd drop the plate. He was close enough for her to smell his scent. It was not the scent of horse and hay she was accustomed to, but of something else, something nice—different—pleasant.

She allowed her eyes to go over him. He was English, and dressed the way the English did. In heavy blue pants that hugged his muscular legs and thighs. His crisp white shirt was a sharp contrast to his dark hair and eyes, and had obviously been store-bought rather than lovingly made by the hands of a wife. The stitches were too coarse for anything but machine work.

"I don't mind helping, Sara, really." Cutter's fingers were on one end of the plate, hers just inches away. If one of them moved a bit, their fingers would be touching.

Sara glanced down at the plate. The thought of just how close Cutter Blackwell's hand was sent a shiver racing over her.

"I...understand," she stammered. "And I thank you for the offer of help. But the kitchen is a woman's place."

She did not want him in her kitchen. Knowing he was there, watching her, would make her feel more awkward and clumsy than she did right now.

She had to glance away because her heart was thudding so hard, her palms were so damp, she feared she could not hold on to the plate much longer. "Please?"

Her voice was more of a soft, breathless plea, and Cutter released the plate, wondering if his nearness had affected her as acutely as hers had him.

Every time he looked into those innocent eyes he felt as if he were drowning in a warm, soft, welcoming pool.

It was beginning to get to him.

"Why don't you go sit out on the porch?" Sara suggested, turning from him and placing the plate in the sink. "It is a nice evening. I'm sure you will enjoy it. There's a lovely swing out there—"

"Will you come and sit with me?" He was standing right behind her, close enough for his breath to feather the hair at her nape, sending another shiver racing down her spine.

"Ahhh..." He was so close. Her mind seemed to empty and words deserted her.

"Please, Sara." Deliberately, he made his voice gentle, not wanting to frighten her. "I'd like to talk to you some more. You did promise Endy you'd keep me company."

She could not, would not go and sit on the swing with him.

Just the two of them.

Alone.

In the quiet darkness of the night with only the moon for company.

There were no elders to chaperon.

A frisson of fear raced over her. It would be scandalous, and if her father found out... The thought almost made Sara's heart stand still.

To sit alone on a swing with a man was a serious matter and signaled a man's intentions. Such a thing was not done without discussion between the families and permission from the girl's father.

But she had no doubt that in Cutter's English

world, such things were of no importance. He had probably sat on a front porch and swung with many women before.

To him, it would mean nothing.

To her, it could mean her good name. Her father's reputation. No matter how much she was tempted, she could not.

Sara sighed. She had to tell him no.

She could never do anything to shame her father, or her family, for they had given her so much. They had taken her in, given her a name and a home and a family. So how could she shame them?

She owed them more than she could ever repay.

And then there was the matter of Joshua, she thought with a weary sigh.

Dear Joshua who had been her childhood friend and nearest neighbor, and alas, also her dearest friend for as long as she could remember.

She had stubbornly and quietly resisted her father's attempts at matchmaking. To agree to go riding with Joshua would have meant that she was considering him as a husband. And if she was considering marriage, then she would have to be baptized.

And be bound by the strict rules of the *Ordnung*.

She'd been stalling, she realized, stalling because she was not certain, deep in her heart where it mattered the most, that she could freely and willingly agree to live her life bound by the *Ordnung*.

Not because she lacked faith. No, on the contrary, faith had not been the problem. She was as devout as anyone in the settlement. It was simply that she couldn't understand all the strict rules of their settlement. Rules that made her curiosity, her yearning...forbidden.

A sin.

And so how could she willingly agree to rules she did not, and could not, understand?

She couldn't.

Which was why she'd been stalling.

But she had not yet found the courage to tell her father that she was not interested in marrying Joshua. Time was passing quickly. Since they were allowed to marry only in October and November, when no work would have to be ignored for a wedding, she knew her father would expect a decision from her soon.

But she had no decision for her father. At least not one he would understand.

So she had been trying to avoid the issue, being too busy with chores whenever her father had suggested she make time for Joshua.

Aware that Cutter Blackwell was standing behind her, waiting for an answer, Sara sighed, resting her hands on the edge of the sink, trying to gather her thoughts.

How could she go sit out on the porch alone, in the dark of night with Cutter Blackwell, a stranger to her and a stranger to her world, when she wouldn't even go sit on the porch with Joshua, her childhood friend?

She could not.

Couldn't even think of it.

Sara's hands tightened on the sink until her knuckles whitened when she realized she *was* thinking of it.

"Sara? Will you come out and sit on the swing with me?" Cutter asked again, his voice a soft, plaintive whisper that seemed to jolt all her nerve endings awake. "Just for a little while?"

Saying a quiet prayer for strength, Sara closed her eyes and took a slow, deep breath.

"Just for a few moments, Sara?"

It was far too dangerous for her to even consider such a scandalous thing. What if her father found out?

"Sara?" She felt the touch of his hand on the back of her *kapp*, as light as the kiss of a butterfly. She felt her knees almost buckle, knowing he was so near and the yearning inside her so deep.

"Yes," she whispered softly, lifting her head and blinking away tears. She stared out the kitchen window at the expanse of darkness.

"Yes," she said again, suddenly turning to look at him. Her gaze met and held his, and she felt that riot of nerves start in her tummy again. She pressed her hand there, hoping to quell it as she gave him a small, shy smile. "I will come sit on the porch and swing with you, Cutter Blackwell."

Chapter Five

As he stepped out the screen door, Cutter had expected to see headlights or streetlights; to hear sounds of life, of living. Instead, silence and darkness greeted him as held the door open for Sara.

The faint hue of the half-moon cast a sliver of hazy light across the darkened landscape. An owl hooted in the distance and a soft breeze ruffled the air as if gently embracing it.

Cutter inhaled deeply, relishing the peace, the quiet and the solitude. He'd had too little of all three, he realized regretfully, watching Sara nervously twisting her slender hands together as if wringing out an old mop.

She stood right outside the threshold of the screen door, the toes of her sensible black shoes primly together, not moving, not speaking, looking at the ground again.

"Sara?"

His voice was soft and slightly amused as he gently lifted her chin until she was forced to look at him. In the dark, her sudden uncertainty—the fear in her eyes—seemed magnified.

"Are you afraid of me?"

"N-no." Even though her eyes were as wide as saucers, her chin rose in a fierce streak of stubbornness he found amusing. "I am not afraid of you, Cutter Blackwell," she said boldly.

"I'm glad," Cutter said gently, letting his thumb stroke the soft skin of her chin, unable to resist touching her again.

Cautioning himself to watch his step, he dropped his hand, knowing if he didn't, he'd want to keep on touching her, and he couldn't afford to allow his emotions to get tangled up in this mission.

Or her.

"You have nothing to fear from me."

The lie echoed hollowly in Cutter's ears, and when Sara shyly smiled at him, guilt pierced him like a dagger. He knew he was lying to her; knew that what he'd come to tell her might just hurt her beyond repair.

"Shall we sit for a while?" Cutter asked, gently

taking her elbow, wanting to erase that doe-in-the-headlights look on her face. "We have one of these on our front porch at home," Cutter said, glancing at the old wooden swing. He smiled in the darkness as he sat down and heard the satisfying squeak.

"In Texas?" Sara asked in surprise, sitting down beside him, but far enough away so that she wasn't touching him. It was enough that she was sitting out here, with him.

If he was any closer, she feared she would give in to the unbearable desire to touch his face, to trace the strong line of his jaw, the high angle of his cheekbone, to stroke the rough stubble of his beard. That firm, gentle mouth.

Deliberately, she blinked away the thoughts.

"Yes." Cutter set the swing in motion, then relaxed, slipping his arm along the back of it. "Have you ever been to Texas?"

"To Texas?" The idea simply tickled her. "No." Laughing, she shook her head. "I have never been anywhere. I envy that you have been many places," Sara admitted shyly.

Turning her head, she looked out over the rolling acres of land. In the distance she could just make out the familiar barns and farmhouses, and farther still, the shadowy outline of the one-room schoolhouse where she happily spent her days teaching.

The sight of all that comprised her life brought both peace and restlessness.

"It must be an exciting life to go and see and do anything and everything you want."

"So what is it you want to see and do, Sara Gunter?"

Startled, she turned to him, and for a long moment merely stared at him in the darkness. "No...no one has ever asked me what I want to see and do," she replied quietly.

Cutter was grinning at her startled expression. "You're sitting there wondering how I knew, right?"

"Yes," she admitted, cocking her head to look at him curiously. "It is strange and puzzling. Here, we have only met, and yet you seem to understand things about me that not even my family or the people who have known me my whole life have ever guessed."

Joshua had no idea how much she longed for, dreamed about. He wanted only a good Amish wife who would bake bread and bear children. To no one could she ever admit she had always thought that perhaps there was more to life.

"Maybe that's because I see things they don't see," Cutter said, shrugging. "Hear things they don't."

"Like what?" she asked with a frown, wondering if this English man had special powers.

"Like the yearning in your voice when you talk about never having been anywhere. Or the wistfulness in your eyes when you speak of being able to go and do and see anything your heart desires."

"And you heard all of that?" she asked, amazed. "But how?" she wondered again, making him laugh.

"How?" He was thoughtful for a moment. "Well, you see, Sara Gunter, you're not the only one who has wanted to go and see and do things. I, too, had that yearning and craving deep inside me." Without another word, he lifted her hand, placing it on his chest, right over his heart. Her hand was as smooth as silk and as soft as a spring rain, and fitted perfectly in his. "Right in here, kept hidden away where no one could see or hear," he whispered.

His deep, throaty voice raked along her nerve endings, jolting them awake. Sara's eyes widened into saucers again and she almost snatched her hand away, the way she would have if she'd touched a hot pot.

In some ways, touching Cutter Blackwell's chest was the same as touching a hot pot for she felt the wondrous warmth of his body even through the heavy cloth of his shirt.

She wanted to close her eyes and savor the moment. Other than her little brother, Josef, she had never actually touched a man. Doing so now was a dizzying experience, she realized, wishing she could keep her hand there forever, but knowing she could not.

Just for a moment, she told herself. For one glorious moment she would allow herself this selfish, indulgent pleasure.

Intent, Sara concentrated on every sensation. The

scratchiness of the cloth of his shirt; the steady, rhythmic thumping of his heart; the way his body heat radiated toward her hand, warming it. The way her stomach muscles clenched at all the strange sensations pulsing through her.

Her own pulse began a wicked dance again, and she glanced at him. "Your heart is beating so rapidly."

"I know," he said.

The touch of his body against hers caused her nerves to tingle. When she started to pull her hand away, to draw away from him in spite of the pleasure she felt, he stunned her again by stopping her, gently covering her hand with his.

"I like the way your hand feels against me, Sara."

Cutter's voice was as whisper soft as an intimate caress, and this time Sara flushed, from the roots of her hair all the way to her sensible black shoes. Having him so close, having his body brush against hers made the yearning inside her grow.

Suddenly nervous and feeling slightly decadent, sitting in the dark with a stranger, touching his chest, feeling his heart, Sara licked her lips, struggling to understand what he was telling her.

"You, too, felt such longings in here?" Amazed, she lifted her gaze to his as she pressed her hand a bit more firmly against his chest. "Deep in your heart? Where no one else could see or hear them?"

Never in her life had she ever expected to find

someone else who felt the things she'd always felt so deep in her heart.

In spite of their differences, perhaps she and Cutter Blackwell weren't so different after all. The thought buoyed her spirits.

"Yep," he said with a nod and a sigh. "All my life. See, Sara, I know what it's like to feel stifled, penned in, longing for something...new...different...exciting."

"Yearning for something you cannot put a name to." She whispered as if confessing a national secret.

"Absolutely. That's why right out of college I enlisted in the military."

"To fight," she remembered with dismay, a slight frown drawing her brows together. "You like to fight?" she repeated, making him laugh.

"Guess that depends on the cause," he admitted, making her frown deepen. "I didn't enlist so much to fight, but so that I could see if I could find what I was looking for, something to curb this...restlessness inside me."

"And did you, Cutter Blackwell, ever find what you were looking for?"

Cutter sighed, realizing he'd never discussed this with anyone. Ever. But he was discussing it with Sara and felt perfectly comfortable doing so.

"No," he admitted with another sigh. "I traveled the world, going from one adventure to another—"

"But this restlessness...this yearning...it was still

inside you?'' Curious, she pressed her hand against his heart again. ''In here?'' she asked softly.

''Yeah,'' he admitted, glancing down at her. A faint breeze kicked up, rustling through the trees like a soft, haunting melody.

''And is it still there?'' she whispered. ''This yearning?''

''Guess it is at that.''

His gaze caressed her face. Her innocence was drawing him in deeper and deeper, and for the first time in his life, Cutter felt powerless.

Sara's gentle ways and innocent nature were in sharp contrast to the harsh, cynical world he'd lived in for most of his life. Her innocence seemed like a soothing balm, easing his aching soul, and he realized he wasn't thinking of the mission or the target, or even success; what he was thinking about was Sara…and her innocent heart.

His hands itched to touch her, to stroke the curve of her cheek, to smooth the worry lines in her brow, to touch his lips to hers, to taste the sweetness of her mouth. He could no longer deny he wanted to touch Sara Gunter. To touch her in pleasure and to give her pleasure.

But it wasn't just her body he wanted to touch. No, that would have been far too simple. This yearning, this need, went far deeper. He wanted to touch Sara's untouched heart and her fragile, frightened soul.

Cutter suddenly realized he was treading on very

dangerous ground. Like a man who looks up and discovers the enemy has him in his sight, he knew he had to retreat, to back off and regroup.

He could do it.

As long as he didn't look at her.

"And so now what will you do, Cutter Blackwell? To ease this restlessness, this yearning?" She looked so genuinely interested he had no choice but to answer her.

"Keep searching, I guess," he said softly, struggling to keep his mind off the sudden ache in his body.

"And will you leave your family again?" Sara asked, her gaze searching his.

"You look horrified by the thought." Taking a deep breath, he dragged a hand through his hair, trying to regain some perspective. "Why does that horrify you, Sara?"

Avoiding his gaze, Sara withdrew from his touch and laced her hands in her lap.

"Sara?" he prompted, resisting the urge to reach for her hand again, just wanting to touch her, to hold her and shelter her, from what he wasn't sure.

Maybe himself.

She swallowed hard before answering him. "Such an idea, to leave one's family to seek out an adventure...or to leave for some other selfish reason is not our way." Glancing down at her clenched hands, she smiled wanly. "For me, such a thing…it is unthinkable."

"Unthinkable?" He raised a quizzical eyebrow. "Why?"

Absently, Sara pleated her apron with her fingers. "Family and faith are the foundation of our lives. The foundation for everything we believe and live for. To leave one's family to seek out an adventure would be not just selfish and arrogant, but a sin."

"A sin?" Cutter repeated in surprise.

"Yes," she said with a soft smile, daring to look at him. "The Amish settlement acts as one. We do not have goals or dreams. Such a thing is *Hochmut*. Pride. Selfishness." She shook her head at the mere thought. In her world, it was simply scandalous. "We accept everything that happens as God's will and ask for nothing more, pleased with the glorious gifts He has blessed us with. We do not indulge in pride or arrogance. Nor do we seek high-mindedness or to learn worldly wisdoms. We are content with what God has provided us with."

She could recite the words she'd been taught for as long as she could remember, but she had never truly felt or believed them in her heart. Perhaps that's why she had been stalling about Joshua, about being baptized, about everything that lay in her future.

"So are you saying it would be a sin to seek out your goals or fulfill your dreams?"

"Yes," she admitted quietly. "And it could have very serious consequences."

"What kind of consequences?" Cutter asked.

"Lots of consequences. Serious consequences. Even…the *Meidung*." The last word came out a hushed whisper, and a shiver of fear raced over her.

Cutter frowned, struggling to understand. "The what?"

"The *Meidung*," she repeated in another hushed whisper. His frown deepened, so she rushed on, trying to explain. "It is…shunning."

"Sara, what on earth is shunning?"

Sara took a deep breath, lacing her fingers even more tightly together to stop their trembling.

As she was growing up, her father had constantly scolded her about her high-mindedness and her arrogance for wanting to learn worldly wisdoms, simply because she'd always had a curious nature. Her desire to learn about the world and what went on in it outside their settlement had always been a source of tension between her and her father.

On more than one occasion her father had called her selfish. Even now, thinking of the harsh word, tears burned her eyes, but Sara blinked them back. Her father had lived in fear that she would do something to cause him shame, something that would result in the *Meidung*.

It was an unspoken fear she still lived with. Knowing she was a disappointment to her father had pained

her as nothing else ever had. She'd spent her life trying to be worthy, trying to do all that was expected
of her by her father, her family and her faith, but
knowing she had always come up short had left her
feeling out of sync with the rest of the settlement.

Feeling odd, and a bit different from the others in
that she did not blindly accept the doctrine. She knew
that deep inside she wanted—longed for—more.
More knowledge, more freedom…more from life.

As the wind picked up again, blowing a few errant
strands of her hair loose, Sara nervously tucked the
wayward wisps back into her *kapp*.

It would not do to allow Cutter Blackwell to see
her hair. As brazen as she was being right now, sitting
in the dark of night with him, some things even she
could not do.

"It is not so easy to explain." She realized that
someone outside the settlement would have no way
of knowing or understanding the ultimate punishment
the people had to endure should they break any of the
numerous rules that framed their lives.

"Shunning," she began carefully, "is when a family or a person is excommunicated from the faith for
going against the *Ordnung*—the rules of the settlement." She hurried to explain. "When someone is
shunned, he is…expelled from the community, from
the settlement. No one can speak to him or even acknowledge his presence. Not even his own family. It

is the same as being…dead. It is the ultimate punishment.''

"Do you mean to tell me if you were to pursue your dreams and goals, it would cause you or your family to be shunned?'' Cutter asked.

"Perhaps. Yes,'' she admitted. "It is always a grave possibility. One we live with every day. It would, of course, be up to the church deacons to decide the appropriate action for going against the *Ordnung*. But shunning is always an option.''

No one in their settlement had ever been shunned, but she did not have to see it to know that it would be horrible. To be cast aside, ignored, abandoned by the people who formed your world was such a frightening prospect that Sara could barely even think of it. The thought of deliberately being abandoned again, but this time as an adult, simply terrified her.

"You see, Cutter Blackwell, Amish children are raised in the faith, to believe in this way of life. We do not aspire for more, or seek worldliness or knowledge. To want more is a sin.'' Gently, she smiled at the grim look on his face.

"A sin,'' he repeated, his mind reeling. What was a sin, he decided, was that Sara lived with such fear.

Knowing it made all his protective instincts rise to the surface. And the anger he'd kept on a tight rein for years slowly struggled free.

He knew what it was like to spend your every waking moment living in fear. He'd done it for ten years before the Blackwell's had rescued him.

It was a feeling he wouldn't wish on anyone.

Least of all sweet Sara.

He'd learned a long time ago, on one of his first missions, that the most effective way to control someone was through fear. He'd seen it work in jungles, in rice paddies and in rain forests. He'd seen it, even used it himself because he knew fear worked; you could control anyone if you frightened them enough.

But he hadn't used fear to control life, but to save it.

The thought that someone—anyone—was controlling Sara by fear made him angrier than he'd been in a long, long time.

"Cutter?" Sara said, placing a gentle hand on his arm. "This is perhaps not your way, I know. But it is ours."

"I think I understand," he said slowly, understanding more than he let on. He suddenly realized just how different they really were.

No, they weren't different, he reflected. Just the worlds they lived in.

He had to stop thinking of this in personal terms, he told himself, and he had to concentrate on what was best for the mission. He had to stop letting his emotions cloud his judgment.

"So, this shunning thing, it could happen if you

did something against the...the..." He struggled with the word, then finally gave up.

"The *Ordnung*," she said with a smile, taking pity on him. "And yes."

"So what kinds of things could cause someone to be shunned? Besides being selfish and wanting to fulfill your dreams. Or accomplish a goal."

"Well," she said thoughtfully, chewing her lip as he set the swing in motion again, "there are many things that could cause a shunning."

"Could sitting out here with me cause it?" It hadn't occurred to him that he might be putting her in danger just by his mere presence. His gaze sought hers and he saw her fear. A shiver of trepidation rolled over him. "Sara?"

Chapter Six

Glancing around, as if fearing they might be seen, Sara licked her lips. "I...I don't think so."

"You don't sound so sure. Could you get in trouble for sitting out here with me?"

Her chin lifted in a way he recognized now was her own bit of defiance. It tickled him to no end.

"No." The word came out firm and strong in spite of her fear. "I am merely doing a favor for Endy. He is ill and asked that I play hostess to his nephew. I am sure that if someone saw us out here... alone...together, it might lead to some talk, but I'm certain I would be able to make my father understand."

"I hope so." Knowing the kind of rules and restrictions she lived with each and every day, Cutter realized that the news he had for her might have a more profound impact on her and her adoptive family than he'd ever anticipated. And ultimately, the ripple effect of such revelations might affect her very life.

The repercussions when they came could be huge, Cutter thought with a sigh. Perhaps more than he'd bargained for or more than Sara was ready for.

Cutter knew now he was going to have to reassess his plan and proceed even more cautiously and slowly.

"But what about forgiveness?" he asked, thinking he was probably being rude, but not caring. The thought of Sara living daily with such fear made his guts tighten with an emotion he couldn't name.

"Forgiveness," she said as if considering. "We are a very forgiving people, Cutter." Her slender shoulders lifted in a gentle shrug, and Sara sighed. "If one has been shunned, there is the possibility that if he goes to the deacons and professes his sorrow, admits he was wrong and apologizes for his misdeeds, that the *Meidung* would be lifted."

"I get it," Cutter said.

He wasn't really getting it at all. What she was describing was not anything he'd ever experienced. Or hoped to experience. It seemed cruel, especially in this day and age.

"And so, Sara, tell me, what will you do about

your secret dreams and goals if you can't ever pursue them?'' He studied her beautiful face, touched by the sadness he saw reflected in her eyes. This was clearly a touchy subject. ''What will you do about the restlessness that lives inside *your* heart?''

''Do?'' Bewildered by the question, she shook her head. ''There is nothing to do.'' Her chin lifted and her eyes flashed.

Watching her, Cutter couldn't help but grin. In spite of her strict, controlled upbringing, Sara clearly had a fierce little stubborn streak.

But then again, so did Colt, he thought, realizing just how much Sara's actions and personality reminded him of his brother.

Cutter was quiet for a moment, thinking. ''Didn't you say that everything that happens, happens because it is God's will?''

''Yes,'' she replied hesitantly. ''It is true.''

''Then if that's true, then obviously God put this restlessness, this yearning, in your heart for a reason.''

She considered his words for a moment. ''Perhaps,'' she said slowly, stunned by his observation. She had never really thought of it that way before. ''But it is said that God gives us pain and suffering to make our faith stronger.''

''And do you believe that, Sara? Do you believe God gave you this restlessness, this yearning simply to test your faith? To make you stronger?''

No one had ever asked her such questions. No one would have dared. But then again, no one had ever acknowledged or noticed that she had this yearning.

No one, except for Cutter Blackwell.

She looked at him more closely, wondering if he did indeed have special powers. On some level it frightened her.

"I'm...I'm...not sure." She was pleating her apron again. "You ask questions I have no answers to."

"Okay, then how about if I ask you some questions you do have the answers for?"

"All right," she said hesitantly.

"If you didn't have to worry or fear anything or anybody, what is it that you yearn for? What do you think would cure this restlessness inside your heart?"

She was silent too long. Watching her, Cutter realized he'd probably frightened her. He was pushing and he knew it, but he couldn't help it. The importance of what he was doing—to his mother, to his brother and ultimately to Sara—wouldn't let him slow down. He'd never been known for his patience and he figured he was too old to start being patient now.

"Sara." In spite of his own resolve not to touch her, he reached for her hand again, closing his own around it in spite of the fact that it caused her eyes to widen.

Now he understood why. Not because she didn't like his touch, if the look he saw in her eyes was any indication. But because she was merely afraid. It rankled on some primitive level he couldn't even begin to understand.

"You don't have to be afraid to talk to me, Sara," he said quietly, lacing his fingers through hers. "I'd like to be your friend. I know that we're different people, but even so, I think we can be friends, can't we?"

"Friends?" she repeated, both fascinated and frightened by the idea. She glanced down at their intermingled hands, realizing it felt good to have Cutter holding her hand. She felt treasured, protected, cared for, things she'd never felt before in her life. "You would like to be friends with me, Cutter Blackwell?"

The thought caused joy to blossom and grow inside her like one of her mother's beautiful prized roses.

She'd never had a friend before, other than Joshua, who was more like a brother. And she could not talk to Joshua about the secrets in her heart for he would never understand.

Looking at Cutter, she realized she did not think of him like a brother. Not at all. Perhaps she should have been frightened, but for the first time in her life, Sara refused to be frightened by something that brought her so much pleasure.

"Yes. I would like very much to be your friend, Sara," he said, smiling. "You know, someone you can tell your secrets to."

"Secrets?" Her eyes danced merrily at the very

thought. She'd never even considered sharing her secrets with anyone, for she knew how she would seem to others in the settlement, others who did not share her curiosity or her yearnings.

To share what was in her heart would bring about only pain and scoldings, making her feel ungrateful and unworthy, something she had felt for most of her life.

"No, don't be afraid, Sara. Friends trust each other and tell each other their secrets." He shrugged. "Everyone should have someone they can tell their secrets to. You can tell me your secrets, Sara, and more importantly, you can trust me."

She looked at him carefully, trying not to acknowledge that he was holding her hand in his. "And whom do you tell your secrets to, Cutter Blackwell?"

He smiled. "My mom and my brothers."

She frowned. "But not your father?"

"No, yes." Cutter laughed, dragging his free hand through his hair. "I tell my dad my secrets, too. We're all incredibly close. But my dad, well, he had a heart attack last year, and so all of us have tried to make life a little easier for him so he doesn't worry. But I tell him secrets, too, Sara."

"Your father..." Without thinking, she laid her free hand on his chest. "I am so sorry."

Her concerned gaze searched his and Cutter felt something warm and foreign wrap around his heart.

She was comforting him, something that rarely happened outside his family.

"Your father, is he now fine from this attack?"

"Yes, Sara, my dad's fine. He and my mom retired to Florida so my dad could take it easy. My brothers and I have taken over all the care of his businesses and land. So my dad doesn't have to worry."

Touched and pleased, she smiled at him. "It is good you honor your father and do the chores he is no longer capable of." Her smile blossomed. "So we do have some things in common. We, too, believe in taking care of our sick and elderly." She glanced at him, finding a boldness from somewhere deep within. "And so, Cutter Blackwell, what kind of secrets do you have?"

"All kinds," he offered evasively.

Like what he was doing here in this small Amish community, sitting on an old-fashioned porch swing with a beautiful young woman who was wreaking havoc with his well-laid plans.

"I have secrets about what I'm buying my brothers for Christmas. And a secret about something special I'm doing for my mother." Although tempted, he would not tell her any more. Not now. Not yet.

Shifting his weight, Cutter stretched out his leg for a moment, easing a cramp and trying to ease his own discomfort at the turn in the conversation.

"So, Sara, what are your secrets? If you wouldn't suffer any consequences, what would you like to do?

Where would you like to go? What do you dream about?''

"And you really want to know these things?" she asked, hope shining from her eyes.

"I do," he said with a nod.

"But...why?"

"Because I want to be your friend, Sara. I want you to trust me."

"I think we are already friends," she admitted. "I have talked more with you about many things, things I have never spoken to anyone about. Except for my baby brother Josef, I do not think I have ever talked to anyone so much."

Or enjoyed it so much, Sara thought to herself.

"Good." Pleased, Cutter set the swing in motion again, listening to the creak echo in the quiet night. "So, Sara, what would you like to do?"

"And you will not be shocked?" she wondered aloud, still unsure about this trusting business.

He laughed. "Sara, I doubt that you could ever say or do anything that would shock me."

"Perhaps you are too sure of yourself, Cutter Blackwell," she said in a teasing voice, pleased when he smiled.

A wisp of wind blew across the landscape, making Sara shiver again.

"Are you cold?" Cutter asked abruptly. Before she could answer, he was already unbuttoning his heavy white shirt and slipping it off to wrap around her, sliding closer to her to do so.

"N-no," Sara stammered, the word evaporating in her mouth as she felt the warmth of his body pressed against hers.

She glanced down at herself, at the crisp whiteness of his shirt, trying to ignore the fact that she was sitting in the dark, all alone with a man who now had his arm around her. And his shirt off.

"Oh, my," she breathed. She had never seen a man without his shirt before. Cutter was a sight to behold. He had broad, muscled shoulders that were a gleaming shade of bronze. And a wide chest, equally bronzed and dotted with a smattering of black curly hair. For an instant, she merely stared, her fingers itching to touch his beautiful chest.

"Sara?" Amused at the shock on her face and the curiosity in her eyes, Cutter tapped her shoulder. "Uh...Sara?"

She blinked a couple of times, dragging her gaze from his glorious chest to meet his eyes. She flushed deeply, feeling the warmth cover her face. "I'm sorry," she whispered, lowering her chin. "I did not mean to be rude."

He laughed. "Sara, there's nothing rude about looking at a man." He lifted her chin. "Nothing rude at all. Why shouldn't you like looking at me?" He didn't give her a chance to answer. "I like looking at you and I'm not the least bit embarrassed by it."

That made her sit up and take notice. "You...you like looking at me?"

Sara couldn't remember when something had pleased her so much, and she absently tucked another errant strand of hair into her *kapp*.

"Of course, you're a beautiful woman, Sara. Why shouldn't I like looking at you?"

"You...you think I am...beautiful?" Such a thing no one had ever said to her before. It made her heart pound as if a windstorm had started in her chest.

She knew better than to be pleased by his words. She should not be pleased because he found her pleasant to look at; such a thing was shallow and foolish. It was sinful to take pleasure in comments about her appearance.

"Tell me about college," she said, wanting guiltily to forget the pleasure coursing through her at his kind words.

"Didn't you go to college?" Cutter asked with a frown. "I don't understand. How can you teach if you didn't go to college?"

She turned to look at him, her eyes wide as suspicion slowly spread over her features. "And so tell me, Cutter Blackwell, how is it that we have only just met and yet you know that I am a teacher?"

He'd spooked her, he realized instantly, watching a guarded look leap into her eyes.

Careful, Cutter silently cautioned himself as Sara watched him warily, her eyes full of questions.

And suspicion.

Damn! He was either getting old or sloppy, letting a remark like that slip out.

He rubbed a hand over his forehead as if deep in thought. "I'm not really sure, Sara," he lied. "I think maybe Endy mentioned it to me while we were waiting for you to arrive tonight. You are a teacher, aren't you?" He tried to feign innocence, but it had been a long, long time since he'd been innocent.

"Yes. I teach at our settlement school."

"But you didn't go to college?"

She shook her head.

"Why?" Cutter frowned. "I don't understand, Sara. How can you be a teacher if you didn't go to college? And why didn't you go to college?"

"Because it is not our way."

Lifting her chin, she dared a glance at him. He was close now, so close she could see the fine sweep of his dark lashes, see her own reflection mirrored in the depths of his beautiful eyes.

"We have no need to go to fancy English schools and learn things we will have no need of in our life." She shrugged, a gentle movement of her slender shoulders. "We are permitted to go to school until we are fourteen. Then we take our place in the family and help with the farmwork. Girls are taught to cook and bake and care for the family. We are raised to be wives of farmers or carpenters, and mothers to our children. Men are raised to be farmers or carpenters, and to be good fathers to their children. Everything a young girl needs to know she is taught by her mother.''

''And everything a man needs to know he is taught by his father, right?''

''Or grandfather,'' she added with a nod. ''We have no need of further schooling or a higher education. All that we need to know we learn from family and our faith.''

She wondered if he could hear the dismay in her voice, or the longing, feelings she had kept buried deep within along with all her other dreams.

''What else is there to learn?'' she asked quietly.

''If you thought that, Sara, you wouldn't have this restlessness inside you, now would you?''

She glanced down at her apron, knowing she could not lie, not to him. ''No,'' she hesitantly admitted. ''You are right, Cutter Blackwell. Perhaps I would not.''

''Would you like to go to college?'' he asked gently.

''I...I...'' She shook her head, sending the straps of her *kapp* flying. ''Such a thing is not possible.'' The dream had been inside her for so long that to deny it out loud almost seemed to put the final death knell on it. This saddened her. Immensely.

''I didn't ask if it was *possible*,'' Cutter said patiently. ''I asked if it was something you'd like to do.'' His steady gaze forced her to respond.

"Yes. Oh, yes," she admitted, nearly clapping her hands in delight. "More than anything." Her eyes sparkled in the darkness. "There are so many books there, so much to learn, to read, to understand. It…it would be like a miracle to go to a school where learning is permitted and book reading is encouraged."

"You like to read?" he asked.

"Very much." She glanced down at her hands for a moment. "It was one of the reasons I wanted to work for Endy," she revealed shyly. "Not that I do not care for him," she added, wanting no mistakes to be made about her intentions. "But he has this huge room filled with rows and rows of books, and he doesn't care if I look at them or touch them." She darted another shy glance at Cutter. "Sometimes, when my work is completed, I even read some of them," she confessed almost in a guilty whisper.

Cutter wanted to smile at the reverence in her voice for something so simple, so much a part of his life he'd always taken it for granted.

Reading.

"Aren't you allowed to read?" he asked in disbelief.

She hesitated, not certain how to answer. "It is not expressly forbidden, but it is…frowned upon." She glanced down at her apron again. "We have no need to know of worldly things. To have knowledge of worldly things might encourage us to want…worldly things."

"We?"

"My father does not approve," she explained. "He believes that my curiosity about the world and my love of books is merely pride and selfishness. He has always disapproved of my desire for worldly knowledge." The last few words came out in a soft, shamed whisper, and Cutter felt his heart ache. "The only reason he has allowed me to teach is because the settlement needed a teacher."

He thought about his own father, his own loving, giving father who had encouraged him to do and be all that he wanted, to experience all life had to offer. Until this moment, Cutter wasn't certain he'd ever appreciated his own father enough.

"And you enjoy teaching?" he asked, watching her face gleam with pleasure.

"Oh, yes. Absolutely. It is the only thing I have ever wanted to do. I love children, love teaching. But I think I would even be a better teacher if I knew more myself." She smiled. "The children, they are very eager to learn. Especially the young ones who do not yet understand our ways."

"What about books?" he asked. "Can't you just buy books?"

She laughed. "Such a thing is not so easy, Cutter. Besides, we have the only book we need," she said simply.

"And you've never read any other books?"

"Once," she admitted hesitantly. "But my father caught me."

"And I take it this book was not the Bible?"

She shook her head. "No, it was not."

Cutter glanced at her in surprise. "Just once he caught you reading another book?" he teased, making her relax a bit. Someone who thirsted so much for knowledge should have been allowed and encouraged to read as much as possible. "How old were you, Sara, when your father caught you reading? And what were you reading?"

Gnawing her lower lip, Sara thought about it for a moment. "Six, I think. About Josef's age, I guess. I was supposed to be sleeping, but during a shopping trip into town with my mother, I found a discarded book. It looked pretty, with a bright red-and-white cover, so I picked it up and hid it beneath my dress." Mischief danced in her eyes. "It was a book written by a doctor. *The Cat in the Hat,*" she explained, smiling in remembrance.

"Dr. Seuss."

"You know him, this doctor?" Sara asked in amazement. "Is he perhaps a friend of your brother, the doctor?"

Laughing, Cutter shook his head. "In a manner of speaking, I know him. Not personally, mind you, and no, he's not a friend of Hunter's, but I have read the book."

"You have?" Thrilled, she grinned. "I started to,

but…'' Her voice trailed off and she shrugged. "I was not able to finish it."

"Why not?"

She glanced away. "One night when I was supposed to be sleeping, my father caught me reading it and took it from me. He warned that my curiosity about worldly things was selfish and prideful. He said I was an ungrateful child, always wanting more than God had bestowed."

"Oh, Sara," Cutter said softly, turning to lean his forehead against hers. "You weren't ungrateful, only curious," he murmured. "And I don't think being curious is a sin."

"I do not, either," she whispered fiercely. "Please, Cutter Blackwell, do not ever speak of this," she pleaded, closing her eyes as fear swept over her. "Any of this. It would bring much unpleasantness for me. Oh, Cutter, please?" The pleading tone in her voice was almost his undoing.

She was genuinely afraid, he realized, and every protective instinct he'd ever had rose to the surface. He wanted to haul Sara into his lap and cradle her close, to shelter her from harsh deeds and hurting words, to let her know that what she'd longed for— wished for—as a child was perfectly, utterly natural. To make her feel as if reading and learning weren't sins, as far as he was concerned.

"Sara, you have nothing to fear. I'm your friend," he reassured her softly. "You can trust me, and you can tell me anything. It won't ever go any further. I promise. Do you believe me?''

It was suddenly the most important thing in the world for Sara to believe him. To trust him. Even though in his heart he knew he was deceiving her.

Sara looked at him for a long moment, then finally, slowly nodded her head. ''I trust you, Cutter Blackwell,'' Sara said, then had to swallow against the fear that trusting this English man had brought on.

''Tell me what happened that night your father took away your book.''

She stared down at the toes of her sensible black shoes. ''I...I cried myself to sleep, and in the morning...''

''In the morning what, Sara?''

''In the morning I still wanted to find out what had happened to the cat in the hat,'' she admitted impishly.

''So you never got to finish *The Cat in the Hat,* then?''

''No.'' Slowly, she shook her head. ''But it was not so bad, really.'' She forced a smile. ''Now that I am working for Endy, I have a chance to read sometimes, and it is very nice.''

He let that information sink in for a moment. ''Okay, so you like to read and you'd like to go to college. What else would you like to do?''

She was quiet for so long he turned to look at her,

wondering if he'd said or done something to frighten her. Again.

"You will not ever tell?" she asked cautiously, and he sensed the importance of what she was about to reveal to him.

"Absolutely not."

Licking her lips, Sara glanced away, feeling as if she were standing on the edge of a great, high cliff and about to jump. "Sometimes...sometimes... Oh, Cutter, sometimes I wish I could know of my birth family."

There! She'd finally said the words aloud. For so long she had kept this secret deep within her.

"That's only natural," Cutter said softly, causing her to shake her head vigorously.

"No, it does not seem that way for me, Cutter. To want something like that, when the Gunters have been so good to me, taking me in when I had no one, raising me as their own, loving me, it seems that I am selfish once again." Miserable, Sara shook her head. "It makes me feel torn inside. I do love and appreciate my adoptive family, but somewhere deep inside me, in here..."

She reached for his hand as he had reached for hers earlier in the evening and placed it over her heart, unaware of how the touch of her small, gently rounded breast sent Cutter's blood trumpeting through him.

"I feel this need to know of them. In here, Cutter.

Deep in my heart, where all my silent longings for them have always been hidden.'' Sara's voice caught on a sob, and she bit her lip, struggling not to cry. ''I know this need is wrong—selfish—that it was God's will for me to come to the Gunters', but still...sometimes the desire for this knowledge is so strong I fear I cannot contain it any longer.''

Cutter knew better than to touch her, to reach for her, because he feared if he did, he wouldn't let go. The need to comfort and reassure Sara was so strong he didn't dare move.

He couldn't get emotionally involved. And he couldn't afford to frighten her. Or do anything that would jeopardize his chances of staying close to her.

Guilt bit deeply into his conscience, the conscience he thought he'd lost long ago.

After a moment, these thoughts dimmed as other, deeper feelings took over. The feel of Sara's soft, warm breast gently curved under his palm. The frantic pounding of her heart.

Cutter didn't speak; didn't think. He didn't dare. He cleared his mind so that his emotions could cool down and he could focus on his mission once more.

For long, silent moments they sat like that.

Everything seemed to still until all he could hear was the rapid thudding of her heart; all he could feel was the gentle curve of her breast. Cutter swallowed hard, trying to regain and maintain control.

Sara licked her lips again, wondering if she had

indeed shocked Cutter Blackwell with her wanton behavior and shameless confessions. Closing her eyes, she tried not to think of what she'd blurted out. She sat motionless, trying not to feel ashamed.

Another sensation began to niggle through her consciousness. A warmth unlike anything she'd ever felt before, not even during the hottest days of August when she helped her mother in the gardens.

Sara blinked, concentrating on the strange sensation. She had never felt the touch of a man's hand until tonight, not in gentleness and not on such an intimate part of her as her heart.

To feel Cutter's hand now, so gentle against her breast, so warm she could feel him through her sturdy apron and plain dress, made an ache grow low and deep in her tummy, an ache that seemed to reverberate through her entire body.

Feeling awkward and uncomfortable, and fearing that she had indeed shocked Cutter Blackwell, Sara struggled to put things right. To explain herself and her actions.

"For so many years, I tried to believe that the pain in my heart...the yearning to know my birth family...was to help make me stronger. So that I wouldn't wonder. So that I could accept. But...but it has never gone away, this yearning." Swallowing back tears, Sara glanced at him. "It is still always here, deep inside me."

She blinked hard, refusing to let the tears fall and

embarrass herself further. What must he think of her? Confessing such things, admitting her yearnings, her heart's desire.

Slowly, Cutter withdrew his hand from her heart, knowing that if he didn't, he might do or say something he shouldn't.

He took a deep breath, trying to keep his mind focused. But the pain, the absolute anguish in Sara's voice, was wreaking havoc with his resolve, his common sense, everything he'd learned during years of training.

"What would you like to know about them?" he asked softly, brushing an errant strand of hair from her cheek, wanting, needing, to comfort her in a way he hadn't wanted or needed to comfort anyone in his life.

Wiping her eyes with the back of her hand, Sara smiled shakily. "So much. Everything. Who they are. Where they are. If they are Amish. Or English." The words tumbled out of her. "And why…why… they…"

"Why they gave you up?" he finished for her, understanding immediately as only one who'd been adopted could understand.

Sara nodded. "I cannot understand such things, Cutter. To give away a child like an old…blanket." She shook her head, biting her trembling lip. "I have always wondered about how and why it was easier to just give me away."

Cutter knew the whole sordid story. As much as his heart longed to tell her, he couldn't. Not now. Not yet. Not here.

He couldn't tell her that although her life with the Gunters had not always been easy, it had been a darn sight better than any kind of life she would have had with her birth mother.

A mother who had walked out on two little boys without a thought, leaving one to die and one who'd almost died in a fire that destroyed their home.

A mother who had gone on to have another child, a little girl she'd coldly abandoned somewhere.

That's when he'd lost Sara's trail, right before her mother had abandoned her. And once he learned about her, it had taken him six long months to find her.

Now that he had, he knew he owed it to her to do this right. To let her know gently and in his own way that she had a real family—Colt—who would no doubt love Sara with all his heart.

Unable to bear the anguish in her eyes, Cutter reached for her, damning his resolve and his tangled emotions. For just one moment, he'd forget his mission, forget Sara was the target. Forget that so much rested on his actions.

And just give in to the need to hold and comfort her.

"Oh, Sara." Cutter slid his arm around her, drawing her close. Sara stiffened at the intimacy, unaccustomed to being so close or to being held by a man. "Relax," he whispered against her *kapp*, stroking a hand down her back. "Just let yourself relax for a moment. I won't hurt you. We're friends, remember?" The lie was beginning to echo hollowly in his ears.

Sara tried to relax. As much as she wanted to feel this closeness to Cutter and to savor the comfort he offered, and she so sorely needed, she knew that she could not allow such liberties.

"Cutter." She had to swallow hard to get the words out. "I am sorry for my outburst. I should not be leaning against you. It is…unseemly."

"No, it's not, Sara," he responded. "It's merely one friend comforting another. Surely you've done that a time or two in your life?"

She thought of the time when their neighbor, Mary, lost her first baby and how the women had all gone to Mary's house to cook for her and to comfort her. When Mary could not contain her tears, they had all held Mary in comfort, speaking God's words to her to ease the pain that would serve only to make her stronger.

"Yes, I have comforted another," she admitted hesitantly. But never had she ever felt the comfort of a man's arms before. It made her feel safe and protected in a way she never had before.

"Sara, listen to me. There are ways to find out about your birth family."

Her head came up and her fearful gaze searched his. "Ways?" Her voice trembled. "What do you mean by this, Cutter Blackwell?"

"I've got a military background. I've been trained to investigate. If you'd like, I could do some snooping around for you and perhaps learn about your family."

"No!" The word gasped out and Sara clamped a hand over her mouth in shock. "Ach, no, please, Cutter. The thought, it is too frightening to me. After all this time, what would I say to them, this family who never wanted me?"

"Maybe it's not as simple as that." He shrugged, wondering if he'd gone too far. Or taken a misstep. He'd always believed in playing the hand he'd been dealt and he had no choice but to do the same now. "Sometimes there are circumstances that are difficult to explain. Maybe it wasn't that they didn't want you. Maybe…maybe they just couldn't care for you."

"No, please?" Sara closed her eyes, regretting telling him. "It would be too embarrassing to have them know that this child they did not want then is now looking for them."

The thought brought a spate of tears she couldn't control. It had been hard trying to understand that she had not been wanted, loved. Harder still, knowing that for all these years there had been no one she could speak to about this pain—this hollowness—in her heart.

"I have no wish to be a burden to this family who

did not want me.'' She shook her head firmly. ''Not now, Cutter Blackwell. Not ever,'' she insisted firmly.

''Sara.'' Cutter was absolutely certain his heart was splintering. If she only knew how much Colt would want and love her if he'd only known about her... ''Maybe they wanted you, but—''

''No.'' She shook her head again, leveling her chin. ''I do not think that I could bear it if they...they...''

She couldn't seem to put her deepest fear that her birth family would reject her again into words. Her eyes closed on another thought.

''And if my father...'' Her voice trailed off. Eyes glinting, she lifted her head. ''If my adoptive father were to learn of this, of my yearning for my birth family, he would never forgive me. And I do not wish to ever make my mother cry again.''

''Your father wouldn't have to know. This would be just our secret. And would your mother cry if she knew how much you needed to do this?''

''No,'' she said firmly with a shake of her head, deliberately ignoring his words. It was far too dangerous to do otherwise. ''Please, Cutter,'' she begged, fearing she'd spoken too freely about matters that she had best kept silent about, ''let us not discuss this.'' Alarmed by her thoughts and her actions, Sara pushed away from him and jumped to her feet. ''It is late. I must go in. I have much to do tomorrow and I have been wasting time.''

Cutter stood, turning her by her shoulders to face

him. "No, Sara. You weren't wasting time." He smiled tenderly, lifting her chin gently. "You were talking with a friend. And I am you friend," he said firmly. "I'm sorry I upset you—"

"No, no. You did not upset me." Wanly, she forced a smile. "It is just some things are difficult to speak of after being buried in your heart for so long."

"I understand. Can we talk some more tomorrow?" he asked hopefully, so hopefully she smiled.

"About other things," she clarified, relieved when he flashed her that incredible smile.

"All right," he agreed.

She held out her hand to him, and he noted it was shaking. "Thank you, Cutter Blackwell," she whispered as he took her hand in his. "For being my friend and for letting me share my secrets with you."

"You're welcome, Sara Gunter."

She stared at him for a long moment, wondering about this new yearning she felt in her heart. "Good night Cutter Blackwell."

"Good night, Sara," Cutter said, lifting her hand and gently pressing it to his lips for the gentlest of kisses.

With her hand still tingling from Cutter's kiss, Sara made her way upstairs, to the small bedroom she had used since coming to work for Endy.

But she knew that this night, like many others, her thoughts would make it difficult for her to sleep. However, on this night, her thoughts would not be about books or college or learning. Or even the family who had given her away because they did not want her.

But about a man.

Cutter Blackwell.

Sara hugged her hand, the hand Cutter Blackwell's lips had touched, as well as the forbidden thoughts, to her heart and quietly cried herself to sleep.

Chapter Seven

He sat alone on the porch for a long time, listening to the quietness of the night. Dragging a hand through his hair, Cutter desperately wished for a cigarette even though he'd quit smoking years ago.

So many emotions were roaming around inside him. He hadn't prepared himself properly for this mission, he realized now. Hadn't prepared himself for…Sara.

Perhaps the situation was just too close, he thought. Perhaps he should have let someone else handle it. But he knew he couldn't have done that. This was personal; this was family. This was for his mother.

And he didn't trust anyone else to do it—at least not to do it right.

With a sigh, Cutter finally rose, then went inside, hoping for some sleep, hoping to put Sara, lovely Sara, out of his mind.

But he heard her voice even in his sleep. The soft, magical lilt of it. The wistfulness, the yearning.

He could still see her—the porcelain skin, the dark fall of hair framing that incredible face. That mouth, so soft and pink, so utterly kissable.

He could still feel the touch of her small hand resting against his heart, making it beat like a drum. And even in his sleep, he could smell her.

Her scent was all natural, all Sara. Even in sleep it teased and tormented him.

He awoke feeling more tired and agitated than when he'd gone to bed. After a quick shower, he dressed in an old sweatshirt and a pair of comfortable jeans, then wandered downstairs, drawn by the smell of food.

Even though he'd been home almost a year and had enjoyed Sadie's cooking every day of that time, he never stopped appreciating a home-cooked meal, not after years of military food.

"So you're up," Endy said as Cutter wandered into the kitchen, nearly sighing in gratitude at the sight of the full pot of coffee sitting on the plain white stove.

The house was at least fifty years old; the kitchen was long and narrow, with two windows at one end overlooking the backyard. The kitchen had been updated some time in the past twenty years, but it smacked of a male living alone. It was clean and well kept, though. Sara's doing, no doubt, Cutter assumed.

The house was almost military in its bareness, he noticed. There were no fresh flowers on the square wooden dining table that sat in the middle of the kitchen. No tablecloth or place mats as Cutter was accustomed to seeing at home. The six chairs around the table were also plain wood, solid and bare. There was a woven rag rug in bright shades of pink, rose and red under the table, but other than that the rest of the kitchen, including the walls and all the appliances, was basic white.

"Yeah," Cutter said, grabbing a cup and helping himself to some coffee as he squelched a yawn, "I'm finally up. How you feeling this morning?" Cutter asked with some concern, joining Endy at the table.

"A little better."

"Good." Cutter sipped his coffee, his eyes closing in pleasure.

Endy rubbed his stomach. "Sometimes I just eat too fast for my own good. But I guess it's just that I get sick of my own cooking, so when Sara's here, I tend to gorge on her delicious meals."

Cutter held his cup aloft. "Well, you make a great cup of coffee."

Endy chuckled, shaking his head. "No, not me. Sara."

Cutter glanced around. "Where is Sara?" His eyes had been searching for her, seeking her out from the moment he'd left the guest bedroom. Knowing she was here and he'd be able to see her again today made getting up worthwhile.

"Out back, in the yard. Tending to the flowers," Endy said, chuckling again. "Guess I made a mess of the garden last year. Didn't prepare it proper for the rough winter we had, so early this morning, Sara went out to try to set things right. She sure has a way with flowers. They'll be blooming seven shades of the rainbow come June." Endy nodded toward the stove. "Sara figured you'd be hungry. She left you some breakfast over there on the range."

Cutter grinned, getting up to go to the stove. He glanced toward the windows to see if he could catch a glimpse of Sara. No such luck.

"So that's what I smelled." Cutter lifted the cover off one of the pots and sniffed deeply. The aroma was heavenly even if he didn't recognize any of the dishes. "What is all this?" he asked with a frown.

Endy turned toward him. "That's corn and egg pie in the big frying pan. Fried tomatoes in the other pan."

"But they're not green," Cutter said.

"No. They're home-grown tomatoes from Sara's mom's garden that they've canned. But I tell ya, they are a treat for the taste buds. 'Specially the way Sara makes them. Lordy, that girl can cook. And there's cinnamon flop still warming in the oven."

"Cinnamon flop?" Cutter's brows rose at the

strange name, then he opened the oven. The sight and smell of the warm cinnamon rolls made his stomach growl. "What the heck is cinnamon flop?"

"Homemade cinnamon biscuits. Help yourself. Plates are in the cabinet overhead," Endy offered, sipping his coffee.

Cutter grabbed a plate and filled it, taking a bit of everything. "You want anything?"

"Nope." Endy shook his head. "Already ate. With Sara at about dawn."

"Dawn?" Cutter said, straddling a chair, plate in hand. "Why so early?"

Endy grinned. "Out here we always get up early."

"Yeah, I guess I can understand that." He took a bite of the pie. "But since I've been home, I've given up getting up at the crack of dawn." And enjoying every minute of it, he thought as he ate heartily.

"So how did it go last night, Cutter?" Endy asked quietly, looking at him carefully over the rim of his cup.

Cutter set his fork down, then wiped his mouth with the paper towel he'd grabbed. "It's funny. I've been on hundreds of missions over the years, and maybe a couple over the years have surprised me, but none more than this one."

"How so?" Endy asked.

Cutter was thoughtful. "Sara's not at all what I expected. Or anticipated. She's a special woman," he said slowly, causing Endy to look at him sharply.

"And that troubles you, does it, son?"

Cutter's brows drew together. He wasn't ready to talk to anyone about the effect Sara was having on him. For now, he'd keep his conversation strictly on the mission.

"In a way," Cutter finally admitted. "With any mission, I pride myself on being totally prepared, looking at every angle, anticipating every eventuality or setback, but this time..."

"Yeah, I know," Endy said with a sigh, turning to face him. "But you've got to remember something, son. She's not just another target. She's a person, a human being with feelings and emotions, and a whole life here. Not to mention a family she's spent her life with." Endy peered at Cutter thoughtfully. "Can't imagine you'll have an easy time of it, finding a way to tell her the truth."

"No," Cutter said, pushing his plate away. He'd suddenly lost his appetite. "I don't know how she's going to feel about the whole thing." Cutter glanced at the older man. "Nor do I know how she's going to feel about my deceiving her. I told her she could trust me," he confessed guiltily. "Told her we should be friends."

"Well, that's a good start."

"Yeah, but Endy, how's she bound to feel when she finds out I deliberately deceived her?" He hadn't been able to stop thinking of much else, even in his sleep.

Emma had taught all her boys about caring, compassion and about being a good person. He'd never intentionally hurt anyone, at least not in his personal life. Professionally was another story. But that was different. He did what he had to in order to ensure success of a mission, and generally if someone got hurt, it was their own fault for being stupid or careless.

"Cutter, listen to me." The tone of Endy's voice had Cutter turning to him. "We both spent enough years in the military to understand that sometimes in order to succeed, no matter what it is in life, sometimes you've got to compromise on some of the things you believe in in order to accomplish your objective."

Endy got up to pour himself another cup of coffee before continuing. "You're deceiving Sara now, not to be hurtful or mean, but to protect her and to give yourself a chance to get to know her better. Doing it like this lets you find the best way to approach her so the news won't be such a shock or so painful. She might be hurt in the end, yes, but these are the cards you've been dealt. Remember, if you're honest about everything else with her, I'm sure she'll come to understand that you deceived her only to protect her."

"Yeah, so my motives are good. It's just my methods that are a little…devious." No wonder he felt so guilty.

Endy grinned, reclaiming his chair. "That's about

right. You know how I feel about this. Girl's got a
right to know about her real kin. It'd be a pity to keep
such a thing from her. It woulda been different if
they'd never come searching for her." Endy
shrugged. "But you have, so now you got to do
what's best for everyone, to let everyone know the
facts, then let them make their own decisions. Especially Sara." Endy paused for a moment to sip his
coffee, then he glanced up at Cutter. "But I want you
to remember the promise you made me the day you
showed up here."

"I remember," Cutter said absently, turning to
glance out the window, hoping to see Sara. How was
it possible that he was *missing* her? He shook his head
in disbelief.

"Cutter, did you hear me?"

He reluctantly dragged his gaze from the window.
"I'm not going to hurt her, Endy," he said softly.

"She's got a lot at stake the way I figure it."

They all did.

It suddenly occurred to him that *he* might have a
great deal at stake here, too, especially his own feelings and emotions. Meeting Sara had had a profound
impact on him, much the same way meeting his adoptive mother had.

The day he'd met Emma Blackwell had changed
his life. And now, twenty-something years later, he'd
met another angel, and somewhere deep inside, Cutter

had a feeling Sara, too, would somehow change his life.

The thought would have frightened him—terrified him—just a few months ago, before he'd ever heard of Sara Gunter. Before he'd spent months searching for her, learning about her. He knew more about Sara than he did about people he'd known for years. In some ways he felt as if he'd known her forever, simply because of the circumstances.

Perhaps that's why she'd been able to arouse feelings in him in just a brief period of time, feelings he'd never allowed himself to have before for a woman.

He'd always kept women at an emotional distance, never letting any one of them close enough to hurt him. Trust had always been an issue in his life. He'd not had much to give, and what he'd had he'd given to Justin and Emma Blackwell, and his brothers.

He had been absolutely certain there wasn't another person in the world he would ever be able to give that trust to. But he suddenly realized that Sara—sweet, innocent Sara—had not just garnered his trust, but a whole lot more.

Tread carefully, he cautioned himself. He knew there were risks with every mission. He just had to be on the lookout for them and adjust his operating procedures accordingly. Piece of cake, he decided, lifting his cup. He'd done it innumerable times.

But deep inside, Cutter had a nagging feeling that

somewhere along the line in this operation, he was about to step into a minefield. Even though he knew it was there, for the first time in his life he felt powerless to do anything about it.

"Cutter, you'd better come to terms with the fact that you're going to end up hurting Sara once she knows who you really are and why you're here. No doubt about it. No way around it. Not with what you've got to tell her. I don't really know how she'll take it. It's bound to be a shock, that's for sure."

"I know," Cutter said with a sigh. He picked up his cup, staring into it for a moment. "Endy, tell me about Sara's family."

"Her family?" Endy shrugged. "What do you want to know?"

"I'm not sure. Anything you think might help me get a handle on this."

Endy's bushy white brows drew together in a frown. "Well, her mother is a quiet, mousy thing. But then again, most Amish women are. Her father, Josef, from what I hear, is a stern taskmaster, especially with Sara."

"Why with Sara?" Resentment rose, and Cutter found his muscles tensing much the way they had the night before when Sara told him about her father confiscating her book.

"I don't know. I've only met the man once when I inquired about having Sara come work for me. He invited me into his house, although I must admit he was a bit reluctant. Like most people of the settlement, he doesn't like or trust outsiders.''

"Great," Cutter said. "So what's so scary about outsiders?''

"The Amish stick to their own. One of their big things in life is not to be dependent on the outside world for anything. That's why they butcher their meat from their own stock, grow and can their own fruits and vegetables, use horses and buggies to get around. And I can tell you this, most Amish don't take kindly to us—English as they call us—but I have a feeling Sara's father's feelings are stronger than most.''

"Why do you figure that?" It was an interesting tidbit, and Cutter wondered if it might have some bearing on Sara's life.

"Don't rightly know for sure. From the way he acted the day we met, I might have been some vile bit of vermin that crossed into his line of vision,'' Endy said, laughing.

"Yeah, but if that's the case, why did he let Sara come to work for you—an outsider—and an English one at that.''

"Practicality, my boy. The man may not like me, but he's not stupid. The Gunters are small for an Amish family, and since the old man doesn't have many hands to help with the farming, he doesn't produce as much as the others. The money Sara earns helps out the family.''

"The family? Does she give the money to them? I mean, doesn't she get to keep her pay?"

Endy laughed. "Son, you've got a lot to learn about the Amish people. Sara doesn't even see the money she earns here. Once a month I drop off an envelope—cash only. They don't have bank accounts or checking accounts or any other such nonsense. I deliver it directly to her father."

"He takes her money?" Cutter's resentment against Sara's father was growing, and he realized it was totally out of proportion.

From everything he'd learned about the Amish, he realized what Sara's father did was pretty much the norm. Fathers were the head of the house and everyone else just fell into line, like it or not. Especially women and children.

Dragging a hand through his hair, Cutter tried not to sigh. It was a way of life he'd never be able to understand.

Sara's family was still living in an age that for most had died years ago. His own family—his mother and father—were totally equal in every aspect of their life and marriage.

And Cutter knew *he'd* never want to have it any other way.

It saddened him to realize that Sara had never known any other way—or that any other way even existed.

"How can her father take money she's earned?" He shook his head. "It just rubs me wrong."

"Cutter, you don't understand, son. To them, it's not Sara's money. Yes, she may have earned it, but the money belongs to the family. Everything they have belongs to the family. There are no individuals in the settlement. Everyone in the family contributes and shares as one."

"Yeah, I'm beginning to understand. It fits in with what Sara told me last night." Hooking an arm over the back of his chair, Cutter stretched out his legs. "Okay, so why is Sara's father so stern with her?"

"I wish I knew," Endy said softly, glancing out the window where Sara walked past carrying a basket with her gardening tools slung over her arm. "I guess old Josef is leery because she's a girl. And a good girl, mind you, but remember, she wasn't born to him, and although I'm sure he loves her, I just think it's not the same as having a child of his own. Like any father, I'm sure he worries about raising a daughter."

"Is he the same with the little boy?" Cutter asked curiously, thinking about the towheaded youngster he'd seen with Sara. "Sara's brother?"

"I'm not sure," Endy admitted. "I know Sara was their only child for a long, long time. And then, oh, I don't know, about five years ago, I guess, they took in little Josef."

"Took in?" Cutter frowned. "You mean adopted."

"Nope." Endy shook his head. "Adopted is what we call it. Going through legal channels and lawyers and such. The Amish do not adhere to our laws, or at least don't participate in them unless they're forced to. I really don't know how they got little Josef, or Sara, for that matter. I don't think Sara knows, either. And the Amish are not too keen on asking or answering questions. All I know is that about five years ago, a little towheaded kid turned up at their farm. From that day on, he was always there. When Sara came to work for me, she mentioned she had a little brother. One day, she brought him with her and I recognized him." Endy shrugged. "But if you're asking me if they went through legal channels to get the kid, I'd have to say my best guess is no."

"Interesting," Cutter said, his mind churning. He glanced at his watch. "What time do you have to be at the doctor's?"

As long as Cutter was going to be in town, he might as well check out the county records, see if there was any official record of Sara's adoption.

Not that he had any doubt she was Colt's natural-born sister. Not after meeting her and seeing the uncanny resemblance. But it might help to know how she'd come to live with the Gunters. If she'd been legally adopted, there'd be some record of it. And if she hadn't been, that might explain why Colt had never even known he'd had a sister. Colt's mother had not been exactly concerned with details.

How To Play:

No Risk!

1. With a coin, carefully scratch off the 3 gold areas on your Lucky Carnival Wheel. By doing so you have qualified to receive everything revealed — 2 FREE books and a surprise gift — ABSOLUTELY FREE!

2. Send back this card and you'll receive brand-new Silhouette Special Edition® novels. These books have a cover price of $4.50 each in the U.S. and $5.25 each in Canada, but they are yours TOTALLY FREE!

3. There's no catch! You're under no obligation to buy anything. We charge nothing — ZERO — for your first shipment. And you don't have to make any minimum number of purchases—not even one!

4. The fact is thousands of readers enjoy receiving books by mail from the Silhouette Reader Service™. They enjoy the convenience of home delivery…they like getting the best new novels at discount prices, BEFORE they're available in stores...and they love their *Heart to Heart* subscriber newsletter featuring author news, horoscopes, recipes, book reviews and much more!

5. We hope that after receiving your free books you'll want to remain a subscriber. But the choice is yours — to continue or cancel, anytime at all! So why not take us up on our invitation, with no risk of any kind. You'll be glad you did.

No Cost!

© 1998 HARLEQUIN ENTERPRISES LTD. ® and TM are trademarks owned by Harlequin Books S.A. used under license.

LUCKY

Find Out Instantly The Gifts You Get Absolutely FREE!

Carnival Wheel

Scratch-off Game →

Scratch off ALL 3 Gold areas

YES!

I have scratched off the 3 Gold Areas above. Please send me the 2 FREE books and gift for which I qualify! I understand I am under no obligation to purchase any books, as explained on the back and on the opposite page.

335 SDL CY4M   **235 SDL CY4H**

NAME   (PLEASE PRINT CLEARLY)

ADDRESS

APT.#   CITY

STATE/PROV.   ZIP/POSTAL CODE

Offer limited to one per household and not valid to current
Silhouette Special Edition® subscribers. All orders subject to approval.   **(S-SE-04/00)**

DETACH AND MAIL CARD TODAY!

The Silhouette Reader Service™ — Here's how it works:

Accepting your 2 free books and gift places you under no obligation to buy anything. You may keep the books and gift and return the shipping statement marked "cancel." If you do not cancel, about a month later we'll send you 6 additional novels and bill you just $3.80 each in the U.S., or $4.21 each in Canada, plus 25¢ delivery per book and applicable taxes if any.* That's the complete price and — compared to cover prices of $4.50 each in the U.S. and $5.25 each in Canada — it's quite a bargain! You may cancel at any time, but if you choose to continue, every month we'll send you 6 more books, which you may either purchase at the discount price or return to us and cancel your subscription.

*Terms and prices subject to change without notice. Sales tax applicable in N.Y. Canadian residents will be charged applicable provincial taxes and GST.

If offer card is missing write to: Silhouette Reader Service, 3010 Walden Ave., P.O. Box 1867, Buffalo, NY 14240-1867

BUSINESS REPLY MAIL
FIRST-CLASS MAIL   PERMIT NO. 717   BUFFALO, NY

POSTAGE WILL BE PAID BY ADDRESSEE

SILHOUETTE READER SERVICE
3010 WALDEN AVE
PO BOX 1867
BUFFALO NY 14240-9952

NO POSTAGE
NECESSARY
IF MAILED
IN THE
UNITED STATES

"In about an hour, so we'd better get a move on." Endy stood up, then paused, laying a hand on Cutter's shoulder. "I know you've got to do what you've got to do, son, and I support it one hundred percent."

"But?" Cutter said with a lift of his brow. He knew a warning when he heard one.

"But what I don't want is you playing with Sara's affections. She lives in a sheltered, insular world. She's not had any experience with males, especially not like us, and she's a sensitive young woman with a tender heart. I care for her deeply, as if she were my own granddaughter. You do what you've got to do to bring her news of her kin, but I won't have you taking advantage of her in any way. I understand what you're doing here, but I won't be so understanding if you break her heart in the process. You just—" Endy's voice broke off as the back door opened.

"Good morning to you, Cutter Blackwell," Sara said, coming in and shutting the door. "I see that you've found the breakfast I left for you." Sara moved to the counter to set down her gardening basket and tools.

Cutter stood, as did Endy, when she came into the room. His gaze seemed to drink her in and he felt that familiar warmth she brought out slowly unfold inside him. "Indeed I did." Cutter reached for his coffee cup. "It was delicious."

Sara glanced over at his plate. "But you did not finish," she said with some alarm. Her gaze went to his. "If you didn't like it, I could make you something else."

Cutter laughed. "Sara, I loved it. But I'm stuffed." He sipped his coffee. "You're a wonderful cook, but I think I told you that last night."

"Yes, you did." She beamed and began clearing the table.

"We're heading into the city now, Sara," Endy said, pushing in his chair and giving Cutter a deliberate look. Obviously, their conversation wasn't finished, Cutter thought.

"To see the doctor?" Sara queried as she set dirty dishes in the sink to soak while she cleared the rest of the table.

Endy nodded.

"And did you drink the cabbage juice I left for you?"

Endy grinned. "Sure did."

Cutter glanced at Endy, his brows rising in curiosity, but Endy held a finger to his mouth, preventing him from asking the question burning his lips.

"When you return, I will have dinner ready," Sara said, reaching for a towel to wipe her hands. "I will prepare enough meals for the rest of the week for you, as well."

"Thanks, Sara honey." Endy nodded toward Cutter. "Well, we'll get out of your way, Sara. You have a nice afternoon." Endy hustled Cutter out of the kitchen, leaving Sara alone.

"Cabbage juice?" Cutter questioned softly, trying not to grin as he grabbed his car keys off the hall table.

"An old Amish medicinal remedy." Endy rolled his eyes, then rubbed his stomach as Cutter chuckled. "Designed to either kill or cure you," Endy muttered as he led Cutter toward the front door.

Sara couldn't stop smiling as she went about cleaning up the kitchen. She had been looking forward to seeing Cutter again this morning, so much so that she had hardly been able to sleep last night.

So many thoughts kept crowding through her mind, one after the other, that when the sun rose, she was exhausted from lack of sleep.

What must he think of her? she wondered as she filled the sink with hot, soapy water, then slid the breakfast plates in. She'd never spoken so boldly or admitted such brazen things to anyone before.

Her confessions to Cutter were part of what had kept her up most of the night. Perhaps, she thought, she'd opened up to Cutter because they shared a common bond—they had both been adopted.

But near dawn, after tossing and turning all night, she realized that it was far more than a common bond. There was something about Cutter Blackwell, something kind, gentle and wonderful that had touched her fragile heart in a way she'd never felt before.

And didn't understand now.

All she knew was that she suddenly had strange, strong and inexplicable feelings for Cutter Blackwell. Dear Lord, she feared she might be falling in love with him.

The thought so frightened her, that Sara's eyes closed and she grabbed the edge of the sink, refusing to even acknowledge such a ridiculous, impossible notion.

Sara sighed. Knowing Cutter was sleeping just down the hall had only made matters worse, causing her to toss and turn even more. And when she did manage to shut her eyes, all she saw was Cutter. His beautiful face. Those gentle hands. That wondrous chest.

Shaking the image away, Sara ran more hot water into the sink, letting it cool a bit before dipping her hands in. She'd never spent the night in a house with a man who wasn't family. Except for Endy, and she supposed that didn't count.

After setting the last clean dish to drain, Sara lifted the pans into the sink, deliberately ignoring Endy's dish washer in favor of doing the dishes her normal way.

Daydreaming, she nearly scrubbed the finish off a pot as she stared out the window, thinking about Cutter. He was the most amazing, interesting man she'd ever encountered. Not that she'd ever encountered many men in her life, at least not outside the settlement.

But still, Cutter was not just different from the men she knew, but he was also...special.

She'd sensed it from the moment she'd laid eyes on him. There was a sweetness about him, a gentleness she'd never realized a man could have. And when he'd touched her—her hand, her heart—she'd felt something open and blossom inside her, something that only added to the painful, pitiful longings deep in her heart.

What would it be like, she wondered again as she'd wondered most of the life, to be married to a man she was in love with? Sara found her lips curving as she set about scrubbing another pot.

Wonderful, she decided. A man like Cutter would treat a woman like a precious prize and not like a...a possession. That was the only word that came to mind.

She had a feeling that life with Cutter wouldn't be cold and dour, as her life and home were now, but filled with love and laughter, and more importantly—happiness.

During the night, growing annoyed with herself, she'd finally sat up in the darkness and scolded herself, realizing she was being foolish, having silly, romantic ideas about a man who was only there visiting and would soon return to his own life and to the kind of women he was used to.

Beautiful women. Interesting women. *Educated* women. Women who dressed in the brightest fashions and could engage Cutter in discussions about his many adventures and travels. Things—all things—she was woefully, miserably, ignorant about.

Resolutely, Sara finished scrubbing the pots, then drained the sink and set about cleaning the stove. She should not be wasting precious time daydreaming about things that could never be.

Cutter had his life. Out there in the wondrous, exciting world.

Sara glanced up from the stove and felt the hot sting of tears burn her eyes. And she had—she had her life here.

A life that would stretch out into the future the same way as it had in the past. Day after day, with nothing interesting happening. Year after year, knowing there was never going to be anything different or exciting.

Not today. Not any day.

Not for the first time in her life did Sara wonder why the thought made her infinitely sad.

As the afternoon wore on, Sara began to worry. Endy's trips into town to see his doctor usually only lasted a couple of hours. But today, he and Cutter had been gone most of the afternoon, and now Sara roamed the house, stifling a yawn, growing concerned.

After gardening all morning, she'd spent the afternoon cooking, preparing not just Endy's dinner for this evening, but meals for the rest of the week.

Now that everything had been meted out and packed away into his refrigerator and the little freezer, Sara was exhausted, probably, she decided, because she'd had so little sleep the night before.

Since she'd first come to work for Endy, every Saturday he insisted she take a break late in the day, right before supper, while he took his afternoon nap. Endy had always told her he felt guilty having her work while he rested. So every Saturday she would get two blissfully free hours to do anything her heart desired.

He knew how much she treasured her time in his room filled with books, and she suspected his dictum was solely to give her uninterrupted time to explore, to read, to merely enjoy.

Normally, she treasured the time, but today, she could barely keep her eyes open and decided to be wickedly decadent and take a nap.

She giggled as she climbed the stairs on weary legs and went into her bedroom. With a yawn, she untied her *kapp* and the small satin ribbon that kept her long hair bound, hanging them both up on the wooden peg rack. Shaking her head, she ran her fingers through her hair luxuriating in the feel of having it free.

When her hair was free, she felt free. Foolish, she knew, but it was her private foolishness and no one was ever the wiser.

Stifling another yawn, Sara opened her bedroom window a bit more, then took off her apron and neatly hung it on the peg rack, then pulled off her dress. Today, she wore a plain black one, which she usually did on Saturdays when she worked for Endy.

The fresh spring breeze filtered in the window, cooling her tired body. She pulled her thin white cotton nightgown over her head, then slid into bed, hoping she'd be able to stop thinking about Cutter long enough to get some sleep.

He was her last thought, his face the last image she saw before she drifted off, hands tucked under her cheek, a blissful, hopeful smile on her face.

Enchanted, Cutter stood in the doorway of Sara's bedroom, unable to stop staring at her sleeping form. The trip into town had taken longer than he'd anticipated, and he'd come up short at the county courthouse. There was absolutely no record of Sara Gunter's adoption, at least not one that he could find.

So he kept digging, asking around town, trying to find anything that would answer the remaining questions he had about how Sara had come to live in an Amish community with the Gunters.

It was almost dark by the time he'd gotten back. When he'd pulled into the long, winding driveway and seen the house quiet and dark, he'd gotten worried. He knew that this area, so close to the settlement, was relatively safe, but still, the idea of Sara being all alone out here worried him.

He'd bolted from the car and torn through the house, finding nothing amiss. And Sara nowhere to be found.

He'd wandered upstairs looking for her and come across her open bedroom door, and now he merely stood, watching her sleep.

Feeling like an intruder, he softly called her name, not wanting to frighten her. "Sara?"

She didn't answer, just rolled over onto her back with a drowsy sigh and pulled the covers up closer to her chin. Watching her, he smiled, then tiptoed quietly into the room.

He stood over her for a moment, stunned. Her *kapp* was off, and her hair, that wondrous, glorious black hair that he'd wondered about, now lay spread across the pillow, framing her beautiful face like a halo.

An angel, he thought again.

Feeling guilty for standing there watching her sleep, he gently reached down and touched her shoulder. "Sara?"

She stirred and a beautiful smile curved her lips, but her eyes remained closed.

"Cutter?" Her voice was a lazy, husky whisper. Incredibly sexy. Unbearably erotic. "Cutter," she said again, making his body tighten as he watched her turn her head toward him.

Slowly, eyes still closed, she stretched her arms

over her head, pulling the thin cotton material of her nightgown over her breasts so that the material caressed the small curves. He could see the tautness of her nipples pressing against the fabric. His mouth went dry.

"Sara." He shook her again, a bit harder now. If he had to stand here looking at her one more minute, sleepy and tousled, looking far too delectable for his peace of mind, he feared he might do something they'd both regret.

"Cutter," she whispered again, her eyes fluttering open. She blinked as consciousness stole through her. "Oh!" Her hand flew to her mouth and she bolted upright into a sitting position. "It's really you?" She shook her head, trying to shake her sleepy thoughts away. "I...I thought I was dreaming."

He grinned. "So you were dreaming about me?"

Her face warmed with heat and she primly drew the covers up to her chin, embarrassed at being caught dreaming wicked thoughts about him in the middle of the day, dressed only in her thin cotton gown, with her hair—her hair!

"Oh, *Godt!*" Flustered, Sara blindly reached out toward the night table for her *kapp,* then remembered she'd hung it on the peg rack when she'd undressed.

"Sara, what's wrong?" He watched the panic quickly steal over her. Saw her frantic hands, then her desperate gaze search the room.

"My hair—you should not see my hair."

"Your hair?" Cutter frowned, reaching out to brush a fall of glossy dark strands back from her cheek. "Why shouldn't I see your hair? It's beautiful," he whispered.

"Ach…" She moaned, then covered her face with her hand. "No, Cutter, you do not understand. A woman's hair…it is her glory. No one is to see it except for her husband."

"Is that why you wear that bonnet all the time?"

She nodded dully, wishing she could dive back under the covers and never come out.

"Sara."

Reluctantly, she glanced up at him. "What?"

"Don't be embarrassed. I promise not to tell anyone that I saw your hair. It will be our secret."

"Ach," she mumbled with a quick shake of her head. "More secrets." Secrets were what had caused her to dream about him last night. And to take a much needed nap in the middle of the day when she should be working. A sudden thought had her glancing around him. "Where is Endy?"

"Now, Sara, don't get upset," he said as he laid a gentle hand on her shoulder. "The doctor wanted to take a closer look at him."

Still hugging the blanket close to her chin and vividly aware that his hand, warm and very male was resting on her shoulder, Sara frowned, trying to ignore the riot of nerves his touch evoked. "What does this mean?"

Cutter sighed. "It means that Endy's in the hospital. It's only for overnight. The doctor wanted to try some new ulcer medication, but he wants to monitor Endy for any complications or side effects."

"Is he going to be all right?" she asked worriedly.

"Yes, he's going to be fine. He'll be home tomorrow afternoon. In fact, I'm going into town to pick him up then."

"And you are sure that he will be fine?"

"Positive."

Relieved, Sara let out a long, grateful sigh. Then her stricken gaze met Cutter's. "Ach, then I must go." Panicked, she started to scramble from the bed. "Now."

Chapter Eight

"Go?" Cutter repeated for about the tenth time as he followed Sara down the stairs.

He'd left the room so she could change her clothes, wondering why she was racing around as if the devil himself was nipping at her heels.

"Sara, I don't understand. Why do you have to go?" Exasperated, he reached for her, laying his hands on her shoulders to halt her movements just before she sailed into the kitchen.

Gently, he turned her to face him. The dim hallway light shadowed her features, making him think of angels again. "Sara, please, tell me what's wrong."

"Cutter," she began carefully, "I am an unmarried woman."

He grinned. "I know that, and I'm damn grateful for it."

Her eyes widened. "Do not swear, please," she scolded.

"I'm sorry," Cutter said, instantly contrite. "I didn't mean anything by it."

"Ach, I know," she said, shaking her head. "I am an unmarried woman, Cutter," she began again. "And I cannot stay in a house all alone with an unmarried man that I am not related to."

"*What?*" He shook his head, certain he hadn't heard her correctly.

"With Endy not here, I cannot stay here. Alone. With you."

"Are you telling me that just because Endy's not here, you can't stay?" he asked in disbelief.

"Yes, Cutter, that is what I'm telling you."

He drew back and looked at her thoughtfully. "Sara, are you afraid of me? I mean, are you afraid to be alone with me."

"I—I am not afraid of you, Cutter Blackwell."

The uncertainty in her voice had him giving her a sharp glance.

"Sara?" He tilted her chin with his finger until she was forced to look back at him. When she did, her face flushed red. "You're not lying to me, are you, Sara Gunter?" He was almost amused at the thought.

"No." She shook her head furiously. "No, Cutter Blackwell—I am not—"

"You're lying, Sara Gunter," he accused softly, losing himself in the depth of her eyes. "Aren't you?"

"Yes, Cutter Blackwell," she admitted. "I *am* lying to you. I am afraid of you," she rushed on to explain, "but not because of what you think."

"And how do you know what I'm thinking?" he asked in amusement.

"Because."

"Because why, Sara Gunter?"

"Because, Cutter Blackwell, I know what you think in the same way that you know what I feel, deep inside my heart, a place no one else but you has ever seen."

That closed his jaw with a snap of surprise. "Excuse me?" One eyebrow lifted. "You want to back this buggy up and run it over me again?"

"Do not make fun of me, Cutter Blackwell," she said. "Do not make fun of me or my life. My life may be simple, different, but I am not stupid." There was a heat to her words that took him aback.

"Whoa, whoa whoa," he said with a shake of his head, realizing what he'd said. "I'm not making fun of you. Nor was I insulting you or the way you live. I wouldn't do that. I wouldn't deliberately hurt you." The moment the words were out he regretted them, knowing they were a lie. He sighed, determined to explain. "'Back this buggy up' doesn't have anything to do with you or your life. It's merely an expression.''

"Another one of your expressions, Cutter Blackwell, that does not have sense?''

"Exactly.'' Cutter blew out a breath. "What it means, Sara, is that I don't understand what you're saying, so I want you to back up and say it again.''

"Oh, I see,'' she said, nodding. "You want to know how I know what you think, correct?''

"Yep.''

"I do not know how I know what you think,'' she explained with a decided frown. "I only know that I...know.''

"Magic?'' he teased, trying to lighten her mood. "Are you telling me now, Sara, that you know magic?''

"No, I would never say such a blasphemous thing,'' she said. "What I am saying is that some things we know without ever being told. Some knowledge is here.'' She placed a hand on her heart. Her gaze searched his. "Do you understand?''

He did, and it made him unbearably nervous simply because he, too, felt the same way. "So what you're saying is that some things you just know about people.''

"No, not people, Cutter,'' she admitted softly, her gaze wide and innocent still on his. "You. Just you.''

Cutter couldn't ever remember being speechless

before, but he was now. He could only stare at her, too stunned to gather his floundering wits.

So he wasn't the only one feeling this unbelievable...connection between them, a connection that seemed to be inexplicable, drawing them together as if it were predestined.

"I *am* afraid of you, Cutter Blackwell, not because I fear you will hurt me, but because...because... I am afraid of you, Cutter, because of what you make me feel."

Her words simply staggered him. The impact of her words landed right on his heart like a pigeon finally finding its home.

Nothing could have touched his scarred, battle-weary soul more than her whispered, unashamed admission.

"Oh, Sara." His hands slid from her slender shoulders to her narrow waist, and he drew her close, but slowly so that he wouldn't frighten her. "You frighten me, too," he confessed grudgingly, causing her to draw back and look at him, her startled gaze searching his.

"But...how could I frighten you?"

"You frighten me because you make me feel things, too. Things I shouldn't be feeling." He didn't give her a reason or a chance to respond. He wasn't certain he wanted to allow either of them a chance to acknowledge what they'd just told one another.

"Sara, please, stay here tonight. I promise you won't regret it."

"Oh, I know that I won't, but—"

"But what?" he asked, still holding her close, enjoying the feeling of having her soft body pressed against his, melding against his hardness. Her chin came just up to his chin, as if she were made for him.

"If anyone were to find out—"

"How will anyone find out, Sara?" He drew back to look at her. "Who's going to tell? Certainly not me, and I seriously doubt that you will."

"Ach, no." She shook her head furiously. "I would never tell."

"So then why not stay? You've already made dinner, right?"

"Yes, but—"

"And your family doesn't expect you home this weekend, correct?"

"Yes, that is correct. But—"

"But what, Sara?" He was going to have to play dirty, he decided. "Are you saying that you're going to abandon me here, leave me all alone while my uncle is in the hospital? Force me to eat a meal all by my lonely self, then wander around the house, doing nothing, talking only to myself? Why, people will think I've gone round the bend."

"What bend?" she asked with a frown.

He laughed. "Lost my marbles...my mind," he clarified. "Sitting all by myself, talking to myself, causing people to point and stare at the spectacle I'll make of myself. It seems to me, Sara, that subjecting me to such a thing would be rude. In either of our worlds. Don't you want to stay here and keep me company, Sara?" he asked softly.

"Oh, no, Cutter, it is not that. I want to stay more than anything. It's just—"

"If you stay, I'll give you your present."

"You are blackmailing me, Cutter—" She broke off. "You bought me a present?" she asked.

"Yep."

"A real present?"

"Gift-wrapped and everything," he said with a grin. Her face was tipped back, and he could see the absolute pleasure in her eyes. He wished he could keep that look in her eyes forever.

"Oh, Cutter." Touched, Sara found her mind warring with her heart. Logic fought with emotion. Looking at Cutter, she realized she could not leave him, not tonight. She would give herself this gift—of time—with him.

Soon, she knew, he would leave, go back to his world and leave her alone in hers. But at least she would have this night to remember, a memory to savor during the night, during all the endless nights of the rest of her life when she would have to face life without him.

"I will stay, Cutter," she said with a smile, her heart soaring as if it had wings. "But only because I do not want to be rude to a guest of Endy's." It was an out-and-out lie and they both knew it.

"I understand, Sara, and thank you for taking pity on this poor, lonely soul."

His words caused her mouth to curve into a smile and the teasing air between them suddenly shifted into something more.

"Sara?" Cutter whispered.

Feeling the inexplicable tension that seemed to be drawing her closer to him, Sara could only stare, unable and unsure of what to do as Cutter lowered his head and brushed his lips against hers.

"Cutter. No." She raised her hands to his chest to push him away, she was sure, but she found her fingers clinging, curling into the material of his shirt, drawing him closer. "Cutter," she managed to whisper, unable to prevent herself from going up on tiptoe to feel the touch of his mouth again.

He tightened his arms around her, pulling her closer to him, allowing his mouth to draw her deeper into the kiss.

The world simply spun, and Sara clung to him, fearing she would fall off if she didn't. It was like a tornado, she thought hazily, swirling and swirling and gathering speed, whirling inside her, tossing everything she'd thought, believed, upside down.

She moaned softly as his lips coaxed and teased hers, firm yet gentle, oh so soft and gentle, making her heart and body ache with a yearning too powerful to ignore, eliciting a whispered plea for what she wasn't certain.

She felt warm, her limbs heavy, and so she leaned into him, clutching him tightly, sliding her arms up his muscled chest, enjoying the masculine feel of him, finally sliding her arms around him, letting her fingers caress the back of his neck.

Tilting her head to follow the movement of his, Sara ran her fingers through the silk of his hair, certain she'd never felt anything so wonderful in her life.

She knew what she was doing was wrong. But the moment his lips touched hers, she stopped thinking, reasoning, and began to feel—only feel—for the first time in her life.

And it was wondrous, glorious, and Sara realized in that instant that all she had dreamed of, all that she had yearned for deep in her heart, had evaporated the moment Cutter had pulled her into his arms and kissed her.

Only two things pierced her consciousness: she was falling in love with Cutter.

And she would lose him.

The thought pierced her heart sharper than the sharpest spear, and she moaned, in pain at first, then in pleasure, as Cutter drew her even closer, until there was nothing but a breath between them, and then she wasn't certain if it was hers. Or his.

All the womanly feelings and desires that had lain

dormant in her heart awakened, demanding to be fed, fueled, satisfied.

Arching into Cutter, Sara pulled him closer so that her mouth could taste him more fully, wanting only to quench this frantic, pulsing need pounding inside her.

A knock at the door had them jumping guiltily apart. For a moment, they stared mutely at each other. Lips swollen, eyes glazed, hearts pounding in near unison.

Sara merely stared, shaken, unable to think, to breathe, still feeling the power, the impact of his kiss and her own emotional response.

The knock came again, making them both start.

"Someone's at the door, Sara."

"I know," she whispered, unable to drag her gaze from his.

"Are you expecting anyone?"

She shook her head, then licked her lips, wanting to keep and savor the taste of him. "Are you?"

"No." Cutter turned toward the door as the knock sounded again. "But we'd better answer it." Cutter yanked it open.

A frightened little boy, Sara's brother, stood in the doorway.

"I...I...I am Josef Gunter," he said, his voice trembling out on a squeak. "I have come for my sister Sara."

"Josef?" Sara hurried to the door, nudging aside

Cutter. "What is it?" Worried, her gaze searched her brother's. "Why are you here? Is something wrong?"

Josef's eyes were glued to Cutter. "Papa sent me to get you."

"To get me?" Sara said with a frown, trying to curb the frantic beating of her heart. She was no longer sure if it was from Cutter's kiss or from fear. "Why?" She shook her head. "I do not understand, Josef. Why did Papa send for me?"

Josef shook his head, sending his long blond hair flying. "I do not know, Sara. But Papa had his mad face on, and he said I was to come get you and tell you to come home." The words came tumbling out, one atop another. Josef paused to glance at Cutter again. *"Now."*

Breathing heavily from the near run home and clutching her shawl tightly around her, Sara hurried into her own yard with Josef struggling to keep up.

"You go into the house, Josef."

"But—"

"No buts," she scolded as she headed toward the barn where she knew her father would be doing the evening chores. "I need to speak to Papa alone."

Josef clutched her hand, unwilling to let go, halting her movements. "Are you in...trouble, Sara?" She could see the fear in his eyes.

"Ach, no," she said with a shake of her head. She forced a smile and touched his cheek tenderly. "Do not worry so much, little brother. I am not in trouble, Josef. I have done nothing wrong.''

Sara refused to believe that kissing Cutter had been wrong. Nothing—nothing—in her life had ever seemed so right.

So perfect.

So how could it be wrong?

''Go now, Josef,'' she urged, giving his shoulder a gentle pat to get him moving. ''It's late and getting dark. I don't want Mama to worry about you.''

''All right,'' he said reluctantly, scraping the toe of his shoe against the ground. Lifting his head, he grinned. ''But will you come up to see me when you are through?''

She smiled, her heart full of love for him. ''Yes, Josef, I will.'' Impulsively, she bent and kissed his cheek. ''Run along now.''

She waited, watching until he got to the kitchen door. He paused, smiled and waved, and Sara forced herself to smile and wave back.

Bracing herself, she pulled her shawl tighter, then walked slowly into the barn.

''Papa?'' Sara called as she saw her father sitting on a small stool, doing the evening milking.

Her father didn't bother to look up at her as she walked closer. Sara took a deep breath, feeling as she always did in his presence. Apprehensive. Intimidated. Unworthy.

''You sent for me, Papa?'' Her fingers clutched the

ends of her shawl until her knuckles whitened. "Is something wrong? Is Mama all right?"

He continued what he was doing, neither speaking nor acknowledging her presence, and Sara struggled not to fidget, not to let her worry show.

"Today," he finally said, still not looking at her, "I had to go into town to buy some new nails. Three-inch ones for the building of the Olfmans' new barn." He paused to whisper something to the animal, then patted the cow encouragingly. "It will be a *goodt* barn. A sturdy barn. And the Olfmans will be grateful."

She struggled not to sigh or show her impatience, but her heart was thudding wildly. Her father had a tendency to take his time getting to the point, believing there was no reason to rush anything. But she wasn't certain she could withstand much more tension. Not tonight, with the memory of Cutter's arms, and his lips still on hers. And her fear and guilt about it making her restless and terribly uneasy.

"Yes, Papa," she said dutifully.

Finally, he lifted his head and looked at her long and hard. There was no anger in his deeply creased face; no bitterness in the eyes that she had forever wished would look favorably on her. His face was a blank slate.

"Sara. What is it that you have been doing?" The question seemed filled with disappointment.

She shifted uncomfortably, wondering if the mark of her sin was showing somehow.

"Doing?" She pretended not to understand. "What do you mean, Papa?"

Sighing heavily, he turned back to the animal. "In town today, I heard that your Mr. Enderly was ill."

"Yes," she admitted hesitantly. "He has not been feeling well the past two days."

"Mr. Enderly is not at home now, is he, Sara?"

Biting her lower lip, she knew she couldn't lie. "No, Papa," she said on a sigh. "Mr. Enderly is in the hospital in town. The doctor wanted to keep him overnight to check him out." She repeated the phrase Cutter had used and saw her father's immediate confusion at the foreign expression as well as his disapproval.

"Mr. Enderly has a visitor. A relative from far away."

It wasn't a question, merely a statement of fact, and she had no choice but to admit it. "Yes," she said. "His nephew has come to pay his respects."

Her father stood up abruptly, knocking the small stool over backward. "You were in Mr. Enderly's house alone with this nephew of his!" His voice thundered around the barn, disappointment and disapproval echoing on each syllable. Beneath his long beard, the mottled colors of anger grew, blotching his face. "Answer me now, daughter!"

Sara's chin lifted, and she saw her father's eyes

darken in a way she remembered from childhood whenever she did anything he disapproved of or whenever he was disappointed. But Sara refused to be cowed; she'd done nothing wrong.

"Yes, Papa. I was…alone in the house with Mr. Enderly's nephew."

"And you would have stayed the night alone with this…this…man you are not related to, this man who is not like us, had I not sent for you?"

She couldn't answer, didn't want to admit the truth.

"Do you not think of your father, Sara? Your family? Are we so unimportant to you that you would do something to shame us with this…this…stranger?" he asked, shaking his head. "This selfishness of yours has been a problem for a long time."

He had lapsed into the traditional German dialect, a dialect she knew from growing up in a house where it was spoken, but she preferred to speak English. Just something else that made her different, Sara thought with a sigh.

Angry at his words and his accusations, Sara took a step closer. She would not feel guilty for what she'd done or what she felt for Cutter.

"Papa, I did nothing wrong."

She would never believe kissing Cutter was wrong. Not even for her father.

"Have you not, daughter?" he asked in a tone of voice that conveyed his disbelief. "*Godt* will judge your actions as He always has." His eyes flashed in a way that had her shivering, but not from cold. "You are not to go back there again, daughter, do you understand? Not until this nephew is gone. I will not have you bring shame to my house. To our name!"

"Papa!" Tears flooded her eyes. "Please, no! You know how much Mr. Enderly depends on me. And now that he is ill, he will need my help more than ever." She was pleading, not just for Endy, but for herself. The thought of not being able to see Cutter again tore her apart. She was absolutely certain she could feel herself shattering into tiny pieces.

"It is finished, Sara. The matter is done."

"But, Papa—"

"Go into the house, Sara." His voice was stern, his words final. The subject was closed. "This stranger, this English, he will only bring heartache to this house. He will lead you away from us and into sin. You cannot trust this English."

"Papa, no, it's…it's not like that." On the verge of tears, Sara refused to give in and cry. How could she ever explain to him about Cutter? Sweet, kind, gentle Cutter, who would never hurt her. And Cutter wasn't leading her anywhere.

She'd willingly gone with him. And would do so again.

"Do you mean to tell me how it is, daughter?" her father demanded. "I will not allow such shame in this house. Do you hear me?" His voice boomed around the barn, echoing off the walls like distant thunder.

"You have brought worry to your mother. Have you no shame for yourself?"

Guilt washed over her for a moment. She never meant to worry her mother or anger her father. "But, Papa—"

"No more!" he bellowed. "You will not shame me, daughter. Do you understand? You will not bring the deacons to my door. Do you hear me?"

"I did nothing to shame you," she said quietly, realizing it was futile. He would never listen to her. Never understand that what she had done was not sinful, or even shameful. In his eyes, in her world, Sara knew it was both.

"Go now," he ordered. "See to your mother."

Wiping at her eyes, Sara turned and headed out of the barn. She was almost out the wide double doors when his voice, as icy as a December storm, stopped her.

"Sara."

She didn't turn around, didn't want him to see her tears. It would serve only as an indictment of her and her actions.

"Yes, Papa," she said quietly.

"This nephew, he asks many questions about you." His voice had calmed a bit.

"W-what?" Certain she'd misunderstood, she whirled around, dashing at her eyes with the end of her shawl. "What do you mean, Papa?"

He sighed, not looking at her. "Aaron Olfman went

into town with me. We went our separate ways to purchase our supplies. When he came back, he told me a stranger was asking about you.''

"Asking about me?'' Confused, Sara shook her head. "Asking what about me?''

"It is not our business what his business is.'' His eyes were dark with something she couldn't identify because she'd never seen it before. "Daughter, I want you to keep away from this man. This stranger in Mr. Enderly's house. Do you understand me?''

She didn't understand anything anymore. Why would Cutter be asking questions about her in town? It didn't make any sense.

"But, Papa, I'm sure that—''

"Away!'' he bellowed again, nearly making her jump out of her sensible shoes. "You are to stay away from this man, and you are not to return to that house until he has gone. Do you understand?'' Her father's eyes glittered ominously. "Or would you defy me, daughter?''

She glanced down. She had courage, but she wasn't certain it was enough to stand up to her father. "No, Papa. I...I will not defy you.''

"Go see to your mother now. We will speak no more of this matter.''

"Papa.''

"Go.'' He lifted a hand and waved her away. When she hesitated, he glared at her. "Now! Be gone with you.''

With a nod, Sara turned and headed toward the house she'd lived in her whole life, her steps slow, her heart heavy, her mind churning.

This didn't make sense, and she wondered if perhaps her father or Mr. Olfman had not understood. Why would Cutter be asking questions about her in town when he could ask her any questions he had?

Certain they had been mistaken, Sara drew her shawl more tightly around her as she sat down wearily on the back step, trying to calm the emotional storm raging inside her.

She glanced toward the barn. She had promised her father she would not go to Endy's again, not while Cutter was still there.

Sitting on the stoop, remembering the way she felt in Cutter's arms, remembering the way she felt when he'd held her next to his heart, when he'd touched his lips to hers, when he'd pulled her close and kissed her until she felt as if a tornado had taken flight inside her heart, Sara closed her eyes on a prayer, realizing for the first time in her life that she might have made a promise she could not keep.

Not even for her father.

Chapter Nine

Knowing her father was watching her, assessing her every move, her every mood, Sara went about her life as she usually did, trying to be the dutiful daughter.

Outwardly, she appeared perfectly normal.

Inside, her heart was breaking at the thought of never being able to see Cutter again.

It was unfair, she decided, to finally find someone so wonderful, only to lose him because of the restrictions of her life.

Although she enjoyed teaching, enjoyed her students, the days seemed to drag endlessly.

The nights were worse.

She would lie in bed, staring at the ceiling, thinking

about Cutter, listening to the familiar night sounds that had lulled her to sleep her entire life. But there was no sleep for her now, not missing Cutter as she did.

What was he doing? she wondered continually. And worse, she worried if he was even still there.

Whenever her mind traveled along that path, it would give rise to a bout of panic that invariably brought on tears. And so she would end up crying herself dry, burying her face in her pillow to silence the sobs so as not to worry her mother or anger her father.

After several days, her father once again began touting Joshua's merits to her, but she turned a deaf ear.

She would obey her father as she'd been raised. But he couldn't soften her heart toward another man when Sara knew her heart belonged only to Cutter.

Cutter was going crazy.

Fearing he'd blown the mission, as the days passed with no word from Sara, he was certain she was in some kind of trouble with her family. And that he'd blown the only opportunity he'd have to get close enough to her to have the time necessary to tell her the truth.

Although he was worried about her, he didn't want to make it worse by going to her house to see if she was all right. That was the last place he wanted to be. The last place he wanted to tell her the truth.

But he would have if Endy hadn't stopped him.

''Son, you don't want to go interfering over there,'' Endy said one night after Cutter had nearly paced the wood off the floors.

''I just want to make sure she's all right,'' he said, tunneling his hands through his hair in frustration and guilt.

Endy shook his head. ''No sirree. You don't want to do that. I know you're worried about Sara, but you don't know these people the way I do. You sashay up to the Gunters' and you'll only make it worse for her.'' Endy paused, then went on. ''Look, son, old man Gunter's no fool. He sees you and he's immediately going to know something's not right. You'll either make it worse for Sara, or for yourself.''

So Cutter bided his time, prowling Endy's house, letting his worry eat him alive. During the day, he and Endy played cards, chess, checkers, anything to keep his mind from dwelling on Sara, from worrying about Sara.

It didn't work. He couldn't stop thinking of her, dreaming of her, and it irritated him to no end.

Sara was trapped in a world she didn't really fit into. Trapped because of circumstances she'd been too young to control.

Just as he had once been.

Well, he was going to even out the odds for her.

Give her a chance at the truth and a chance at freedom. A chance to make her own decisions; her own choices.

As soon as he figured out how to see her.

The days continued to drag.

When the boredom got too bad, he'd drive into town just to get out of the house and do some additional investigating into Sara's background.

He'd learned little more about Sara, but one afternoon he discovered that Sara and Colt's mother was born right across the border in Indiana.

How she came to Blackwell, Texas, with two little boys, or ended up in a small Amish town in southern Illinois was still a mystery. But the fact that she was born and raised right across the state border gave him the first tidbit of news he'd had in a long time.

On the way home from his trips into town, he found himself parking on a road that allowed him a glimpse of the schoolhouse where Sara taught.

Day after day, he'd stand beside his car, watching the children pile out promptly at three, whooping and hollering like kids everywhere, grateful to be free of school for the day.

Exactly forty-five minutes later, he'd see Sara emerge, *kapp* in place, shawl wrapped around her plain dress, as she started the walk home.

He could see her, but he'd spent too many years on reconnaissance to be seen when he didn't want to.

He needed to come up with some kind of plan, he realized. A plan that would allow him to see Sara, to accomplish his mission and yet not put her in jeopardy with her family or the settlement.

He didn't want to be the cause of that.

The first time he caught sight of her, it took every ounce of self-control not to run to her and scoop her up in his arms. To call her name simply to watch that glorious smile light up her face.

For her sake, he knew he couldn't do that. But seeing her brought forth a flood of emotions so strong he thought he'd surely choke on them. He'd never thought himself capable of such strong feelings before.

Except for his family.

And now, for Sara.

He couldn't go on like this, being unable to even see her, talk to her. He was almost out of his mind with worry about her.

He knew he'd have to find a way to see her.

Not just for personal reasons, he rationalized, in spite of the ache of longing in his heart; his mission wasn't finished yet.

After doing some more investigating in the small Indiana town where Colt and Sara's mother had been born, he learned that she had married a local boy right out of high school, and they'd moved to Texas so Colt's father could take a job on an oil rig.

Colt's father left his family a few years after they

arrived in Texas. By then both Colt and his brother had been born.

After the fire, Colt's mother had been charged with child neglect and abandonment, but she simply disappeared. The police couldn't find her and she never tried to claim Colt.

She somehow ended up back in the midwest. And she'd given birth to another child: a little girl, Sara. What he didn't know was how Sara came to live with the Gunters.

It was still a mystery, one he'd have to keep digging into, but after almost two weeks of biding his time, Cutter knew the time had come to talk to Sara.

He drove toward the settlement, pulling over near the schoolhouse, parking his car in such a way that it was hidden from view behind a stand of trees.

In a few moments, the doors flew open and the children poured out. He waited until each and every one of them was out of sight before heading toward the school. He didn't bother to knock; he merely pulled the door open, shutting it quietly behind him.

And then he saw her.

Her arms were filled with books when she looked up and saw him silhouetted in the doorway. Her mouth fell open in shock, and the woebegone expression in her eyes changed like quicksilver to unmitigated joy.

"Cutter!" Sara exclaimed, launching herself at

him, letting the books tumble from her arms to land haphazardly on the floor.

"Sara, Sara." He caught her in his arms, hauling her close and off her feet, wrapping his arms tightly around her.

"I've missed you so," she whispered, framing his face with her hands. Joy washed over her like fresh spring rain, seeping into her pores, invading her heart, her spirit.

Unable to resist, she began peppering his face with kisses, no longer shy about her feelings for him.

"Oh, Cutter." Tears flooded her eyes as she clung to him. "I was so afraid I wouldn't see you again. So afraid you'd left," she said as his mouth sought hers.

With a moan, Sara went up on tiptoe to wrap her arms around him, certain she would die if she did not feel his heart beating next to hers once more.

Clinging to him, she allowed his mouth to take her back to that magical place where the world spun, tossing her about, leaving her breathless, dizzy and aching for more. Greedily, she savored each and every moment, wanting it to last forever.

But she had to be practical.

And careful.

Slowly, reluctantly, she drew back from him, then returned once more to dip her mouth against his, savoring the taste of him, before pulling away and rubbing her hands up his arms, grateful just for the feel of him.

He was strong, solid, and he was right there in front of her, and she would be grateful for that if nothing else.

"What…what are you doing here?" Her gaze lovingly went over his face, the face that had haunted her dreams, leaving her weepy and exhausted.

"I had to see you." He framed her face with his hands, gently stroking his thumbs over her cheeks, pushing back a few errant tendrils of hair. "I couldn't wait any longer." He pulled her close for another quick hug. "I've missed you so much."

"And I you, Cutter Blackwell." She laid a hand to his heart, pleased to find it was pounding as hard as hers. "I have missed you more than I thought possible."

"Sara, what happened that day your brother came for you? Did you get into trouble with your family?"

She avoided his gaze, glancing down at her shoes. "No. Not trouble. Exactly."

He crooked his finger under her chin and lifted it. "Then what, exactly?"

"My father…he heard that Endy was in the hospital—Endy! *Mein Godt!*" Her hand went to her mouth and her gaze searched his. She shook her head disgusted that she had not even inquired about her friend. "Endy, I have not inquired how he is."

Cutter smiled. "He's fine, Sara. Just fine. He's home now and doing well."

Relieved, she nodded. "Good. This is good."

"Now I want to know about you. Tell me what happened."

She flushed, fidgeted, embarrassed at having to tell him. Finally, she took a deep breath and plunged in. "My father was in town to purchase supplies and heard that Endy was ill, that you were staying at his house."

"And?"

Sara swallowed, trying not to be nervous, trying not to be frightened, knowing what she was doing was very risky. If her father found out Cutter was here—no, she wouldn't let her train of thought go there. She would enjoy this moment for as long as it lasted and then—like all the others she had shared with Cutter—savor it.

"And he asked if I was planning on staying in the house with you—a man not of my faith, a man I am not related to."

"What did you say?"

Sara shrugged, her slender shoulders moving restlessly. "I did not have a chance to say much. My father ordered me not to go to Endy's again until you had left."

"Ordered? Sara, you're a grown woman. How can he order you to do anything?"

"He is my father," she explained simply, knowing anyone in her world would understand; but Cutter, however, would not.

"Yes, your father, Sara, not your jailer," Cutter said.

"I think he is afraid," she whispered.

"Afraid? Afraid of what? Of me? He doesn't even know me. How could he be afraid of me?"

"No, not of you, Cutter. Of..." How could she explain about her father's fears of anything that was not Plain, or part of his own world.

"You mean he's afraid because I'm not Amish?"

"Yes," she admitted softly. Reluctantly, she raised her gaze to his. "He wants me to go riding with Joshua."

"Who the hell is Joshua?" Cutter demanded, his eyes darkening.

Sara watched him in amazement. She had never seen him angry before. Love had her smiling, laying a hand on his cheek. "Are you jealous, Cutter Blackwell?" Touched, she stroked his cheek, more pleased than she believed possible.

"No—yes—I don't know," Cutter said, sounding frustrated. "So who is this Joshua?" he demanded again.

"Joshua is a childhood friend." She frowned, staring at the buttons on Cutter's shirt. "And my father thinks he would make a fine husband for me," she finished softly.

"Your father again," he muttered. "And how do you feel about this Joshua, Sara? Do you love him?"

She hesitantly lifted her gaze to him, her heart in

her eyes. She caressed his cheek, then smiled sadly. "Love had nothing to do with marriage, Cutter."

One eyebrow arched at her words. "Excuse me?"

"Respect, duty, honor—these are the only important things in a marriage, Cutter."

"Don't let my parents hear you say that, Sara," he warned.

"And your parents, are they in love, then?" The thought had her smiling.

"Absolutely. Even after all these years of marriage, you can't look at one without seeing the love for the other. Sara, what you said about marriage. You can't actually believe that, can you?" He shook his head. "You can't believe that that's all there is to marriage."

Wanly, she smiled. "No," she said softly. "Something else that would displease my father." Nervously, she licked her lips. "I have always believed that marriage should be to someone you love with not just your heart, but your soul, your...everything." Until she'd met Cutter, she wasn't certain such a thing was possible. Now she knew it was. "But in my world, such thoughts would be considered foolish and frivolous."

"Sara, do you love this Joshua?" Cutter asked carefully. "I mean, do you want to marry this guy?"

"Joshua is a good and fine man, Cutter. And I have always loved him. Like a brother," she added quickly when she saw the dark look sweep across his face.

"But I cannot and will not marry him, not even to please my father." She shook her head fiercely. "I cannot marry a man I do not love."

Not when her heart, her love, belonged to Cutter.

"Can your father force you to marry this guy?"

Sara blew out a sigh. "Ach, I do not know," She admitted truthfully. "Maybe. Probably." She shrugged, not really certain of anything anymore. "My father does not want me to disgrace him or the family."

"So you'd do it so as not to disappoint your father?" Cutter questioned.

Biting her lip, she glanced away, unable to answer, allowing the tears she'd been trying to hide escape.

"Shh, come here, baby," he whispered, drawing her close and cradling her in his arms.

Nestled against Cutter's warmth, Sara clutched the front of his shirt, burying her face in his chest, accepting, needing, the comfort of him. Only him.

"Oh, Cutter, what am I to do?" she cried, her voice muffled. "I cannot love a man simply because my father decrees it. I have tried to be a good daughter. I have tried so hard to do that which pleases him, but I—I—"

"Shh, Sara, don't, please," he said, touching his lips to her forehead, her cheeks, her eyes, finally settling on her lips.

Wanting to drown in the taste of him, to block out

all her fears, Sara closed her eyes against an assault of tears, clinging to Cutter tightly.

She had not known it was possible to love this much, to love so that your heart felt full, overflowing with a joy that was too big, too wild to contain. She had not known that kissing a man, touching him, could bring about a peace as well as a restlessness deep inside that made her ache, for what, she was not sure.

How could this kind of feeling, this love, be so wrong? she wondered as Cutter continued to pepper her face with sweet, gentle kisses.

It could not, she realized, sliding her arms around him. Not even her father or her faith could convince her of that.

"Sara." Cutter drew back, wiping away her falling tears with a thumb. "You are a good daughter," he insisted. "You're a wonderful daughter and a wonderful person."

"No, I have not been a wonderful daughter," she admitted sadly, struggling to stop the tears she'd held inside for so long from escaping. "I have never been able to do things in a way that pleases my father."

"That's his problem, then," Cutter said with some heat. "Not yours."

She glanced up at him, her heart filled with love. "Oh, Cutter, the things you say. They touch my heart and make it swell." She reached for his hand and placed it on her heart again.

Cutter's mouth went dry at the feel of her small firm breast under his hand. His body rioted; his heart tumbled. Closing his eyes, he muttered an oath.

How was he supposed to remain detached? To keep things under control when she kept touching his heart in ways he'd never believed possible?

"Sara." How he managed to say anything was a mystery. What this woman was doing to him, physically and emotionally, was something totally foreign to him. He only knew that he'd never felt anything so perfect, so right, before. Nothing had ever quelled that intense restlessness that had lived inside him for so long.

It scared him to death.

But he couldn't dwell on his own fears now. He had to concentrate on Sara. Sweet Sara.

"I can't touch you, not right now." Drawing a deep breath to steady himself, Cutter looked at her. Reluctantly, he withdrew from her, knowing if he didn't, with the way he was feeling, he'd end up doing something they both might regret.

Her panicked gaze flew to his. "You no longer like touching me, Cutter Blackwell?"

He barely managed a laugh. "No, Sara. It's that I like touching you too much." Blowing out a breath, trying to regain some control, he dragged a shaky hand through his hair. "But we need to talk. I need to see you. Do you understand?"

"Yes, Cutter, I understand."

His mind raced. "Now I know you made a promise to your father and I don't want you to break that promise."

"But how—"

He lifted his hands to her shoulders. "Listen to me. I think I have a way around this. You promised your father you would not go to Endy's house while I was still there, right?"

"Yes, but—"

"So here's what we'll do." Years of planning allowed his mind to function at a quickened pace. He knew if her father was planning to hitch her up with some Amish guy, then Sara would have to be baptized, would have to pledge her life to the settlement.

And Cutter knew he couldn't let her do that. Not until she knew the truth about why he was there and who he really was.

More importantly, who she really was.

She didn't belong here, he realized with sudden clarity. That's why it had been so hard for her to believe, to adapt, to understand and accept all the settlement's ways. He had to let her know she wasn't unworthy; she simply wasn't one of them.

It was that simple.

Knowing he could give her that freedom from guilt, from shame, made his determination all the more powerful.

He had to give her the chance. She deserved to know who she was and to make her own decisions about her life, not have them forced down her throat by and overbearing father who didn't have a clue about who she really was or what she really wanted out of life.

The time bomb that had been slowly ticking ever since he'd arrived was about to blow up—in his face—if he didn't do something quick.

And Cutter knew he had no choice. He was going to have to tell Sara the truth. And soon.

But he didn't want to do it standing in the middle of the schoolhouse when they were rushed and she was hurt, frightened and looking more vulnerable than any woman had a right to. He needed time, time to explain exactly why he was there; to let her know the truth so she could take charge of her own future.

He wouldn't let her get hurt. Especially after what had happened. He wanted to make sure he did this as carefully as possible.

All that mattered to him now, he realized, was that Sara not be hurt.

It was time to bring this mission to a conclusion. But he still needed a day to two to tie up some loose ends.

"You're supposed to come to Endy's this weekend, right?"

"Yes," she said hesitantly. "Oh, Cutter, no!" She shook her head, clutching his shirt tighter. "Please, do not leave. Not now. Not because of me. I could not bear such a thing,'' she said as tears burned her eyes.

"Don't cry, Sara." Cutter covered her hands with his, raising them both to his lips to kiss them tenderly. "I'm not leaving, Sara, not yet. But I'm going to pretend to leave. I'll make sure that my leaving gets noticed so your father thinks I'm gone."

Her brows drew together. "I think I understand, Cutter, but I—I still cannot come to Endy's, not if you're still really there." Her gaze searched his. "That would make my promise a lie, Cutter, and I have never lied to my father." Her chin lifted. "I have never lied to anyone. It is not our way. Do you understand?"

He nodded, wondering how her father, her family, could be so blind. How could they not see her inherent goodness? It was a crime, he thought. He'd met a lot of people during his travels, had known a lot of women, but none had ever affected him the way Sara had.

She was, he realized, one of a kind.

"I understand. You promised you wouldn't go to Endy's while I was there, right? So what if you don't go to Endy's? Why can't you meet me somewhere else?"

"Meet you?" she asked in confusion. "Where would I meet you, Cutter?"

He shrugged. "I don't know. What about that big meadow just behind Endy's house? It's secluded and private, and I doubt if anyone from the settlement will be out wandering around on a Friday night.''

"No, you are right. My people rarely leave the settlement, especially to wander around an English man's meadow in the darkness.''

Her teasing made him smile, and he realized just how much he'd missed her and that glorious smile.

"We'll have a picnic," he said, improvising on the spot. "Just you and I." He grabbed her hands, held them tightly on his. "We need to talk, Sara.''

"I know." She nodded, glancing nervously at the door.

"What?" Cutter turned toward the door, as well.

"Josef will be coming back soon to escort me home. I don't—I don't—''

"I get the picture," he said hurriedly, drawing her close for a last kiss, making her head spin once again. "I'll wait for you in the meadow after dinner," he whispered urgently, clasping her hands tightly in his. "You'll come, Sara? Please say you'll come.''

"Oh, yes, Cutter Blackwell," she said breathlessly as she lifted her face for another kiss. "I will come.''

He took her mouth passionately, possessively, recklessly, hauling her to him until there was nothing between them but their twin beating hearts, sliding his hands to the soft curve of her hips, her buttocks, pulling her softness to nestle against his hardness, wanting to imprint her with his mark, to know that he was the only man allowed to touch her, to possess her this way.

The fierce bit of jealousy that had risen up at the thought of another man—any man—touching her hadn't left and he clung to her tightly, feeling as if he'd lose her if he let her go.

Breathless by the power of his kiss, the unbridled passion that he'd finally unleashed, Sara match him greed for greed, pouring all the love in her heart into this last kiss, knowing that their time together was growing shorter.

And she couldn't bear to face it. To lose him. Not knowing that she loved him. Loved him. A forbidden man from a forbidden world.

Forbidden to her.

When he drew away from her, Sara's eyes were dreamy, her mouth curved in a tender smile. Reverently, she touched a hand to her mouth. "Thank you, Cutter Blackwell, for giving this to me," she whispered. "Thank you."

I love you, she yearned to say, but she knew she could not say the words aloud. Not now. Such a thing would be futile and only become a burden to him. He was an honorable man and would feel a sense of responsibility as well as guilt.

She felt enough for both of them; she would not give him this burden to shoulder, as well.

"You're welcome." He gave her another quick kiss before heading for the door. "Oh, I almost forgot.'' He stopped and turned toward her, reaching into the back of his shirt to pull out a thin, flat package. ''Your present.'' he said, tossing it to her.

''Oh, Cutter!'' Eyes bright, she caught it, surprised that he had even remembered. ''Thank you, Cutter Blackwell,'' she whispered, hugging it tightly to her breast. ''But you need not buy me presents.''

''I know that,'' he said as he opened the door and glanced around. ''Need has nothing to do with it. I wanted to.'' He blew her a kiss. ''I'll see you Friday,'' he said as he left.

Mesmerized, Sara ran her hands lovingly over the present, then slowly unwrapped it so that she did not ruin the beautiful foil paper.

''Oh, Cutter,'' she whispered, her vision blurring as her gaze landed on her precious present. Reverently, she smoothed her hands over the colorful lettering on the book cover, sniffling as she started to smile, a smile that turned into a wonderful laugh.

She hugged the children's book tightly to her, letting her tears fall. At last she would finally know what happened to the cat in the hat.

Sniffing, Sara glanced through one of the windows, hoping for one last glance of Cutter, but he was gone. With a sigh, still clutching her precious book, Sara went about finishing her chores for the day.

It wasn't until she heard Josef's voice calling her that she realized in her excitement at seeing Cutter, she had forgotten to ask him about what her father had told her—Cutter's asking questions about her in town.

Friday, she thought dreamily, grabbing her shawl, then hiding her new book in the bookcase along with the others so that no one would take notice.

She would remember to ask Cutter on Friday.

Chapter Ten

The spring rains finally came, drenching the earth, cleansing the air.

It rained for the rest of the week. But by Friday, the sky cleared, the sun rose, spreading hues of gold and orange across the landscape, making the world seem fresh and new.

Nearly breathless with anticipation, Sara rushed through her chores after school, hurriedly helped her mother with dinner, grabbed the straw basket full of food she had packed that morning just as is she was going to Endy's and headed toward the meadow.

The niggling guilt that had been plaguing her all week since she made her secret plans with Cutter was not enough to stop her from going to meet him. Because she knew deep in her woman's heart—had known since the day he'd shown up at the schoolhouse—that he was leaving.

She wasn't certain she could bear it, but she knew she had no choice in the matter. Cutter was going to leave her, go back to his world. And he was going to leave her—alone—in hers.

Knowing it, and nearly devastated by it, she wanted to have this time with him; this time to remember what life could be like with a man that she loved. Never again in her sheltered life would she ever have the opportunity to experience such love with a man, or for a man.

Duty, respect, honor.

She would have all those things, she knew, but she also knew that after Cutter it would never be enough.

But she refused to dwell on it, wanting only to savor the glorious gift she'd been given. For she truly believed in her heart that everything that happened *was* God's will, and so she had to believe that God, in his ultimate wisdom, had brought Cutter to her.

As she crested the top of the meadow that overlooked Endy's property, a meadow that was heavily perfumed with a kaleidoscope of wildflowers swaying in the early evening breeze, she could see him standing in the distance, pacing, anxiously waiting for her.

When he looked up and saw her, her heart felt as if it would burst free of her chest.

Clutching the basket, Sara ran. He met her halfway, sweeping her up in his arms, swinging her around, holding her so tightly she feared she could not breathe, nor did she care.

"Cutter." Breathless, she let the basket slide harmlessly to the ground, then wrapped her arms around him, clinging to him. "I've missed you. I've missed you." She clung to him, pressing her lips anywhere she could reach. His neck, his jaw, his cheek, savoring the touch, the taste, the mere scent of him.

"I missed you, too, Sara," he said as his mouth found hers.

Her mouth opened under his, and she moaned softly, threading her fingers through the silk of his hair as she drew him closer. Everything female in her responded to his touch, his kiss, his absolute maleness, and she arched her body against him until they fitted together perfectly.

She felt his hands slide the length of her spine, caress the curve of her hips, her buttocks, his touch so gentle as to be reverent.

Her body grew liquid, languid, and she pressed closer to him, wanting to ease the sudden tingling in her breasts; the heated throbbing that seemed to grow and swell between her legs. Letting the feelings overtake her, she clung to him, soft moans escaping her at each new sensation.

Cutter was breathing hard, his body aching, when

reality reared its ugly head and he realized he had to slow things down.

No, he had to stop things.

Now.

As much as he wanted Sara, he realized it wasn't possible. Not for him. And especially not for her. He couldn't—wouldn't—do that to her. He knew what making love to a man she was not married to, one who was not of her faith or her world, could mean.

The shunning.

He'd never abandon her to that.

Never.

Reluctantly, he let her go, then took her hand in his to lead her to the blanket he'd spread out for the picnic supper. Right under a towering oak that was just beginning to regain its leaves after the cold, barren winter.

"Any problems?" he asked, trying to regain some control.

"No. You made such a commotion about leaving your uncle's, everyone in the settlement thinks that you have gone," she said, rising on her knees and throwing her arms around his neck. "Ach, Cutter, I am so glad to see you. So glad we can have this time together."

He held her for a moment, feeling the womanly softness of her, and his control wavered again.

Just for a moment, he thought, burying his face in hr neck, savoring the sweet, fresh scent of her. He stroked a hand down the back of her *kapp,* wishing her hair were free so he could stroke the glorious strands.

As if reading his thoughts, Sara drew back, a shy smile on her face, and slowly lifted her *kapp* off, letting it fall to the ground.

"Sara, you don't have to—"

"Shh." She pressed her fingers to his lips. "This is our private time. No one is here, Cutter. No one can see or know." She removed the *kapp,* then shook her hair loose. "I want to, Cutter. I want to."

"Your hair is so beautiful." He stroked a hand down it, then quickly retreated, fearing he couldn't control himself if he kept touching her. "Like you."

She blushed, then smiled. "Thank you, Cutter."

"Did you like your present?" he asked mischievously, poking around in the supper basket to see what she'd brought. He'd stay busy, keep his mind on anything but the ache in his loins and the sudden ache in his heart at what he was about to do.

"Ach, Cutter, you must think I have no manners." She pressed her hands to her face, but she was beaming when she removed them. "I loved my present. Such a fine thing it was to give to me. But presents are not necessary."

"I know, Sara," he said, pulling free a pile of succulent green grapes and plucking one to pop into his mouth. He was trying to keep his hands off her. "But I wanted to."

He fed her a grape, then watched her laugh as a drop of juice dribbled down her chin. He kissed the spot where the sweet taste of the grape juice remained. Her eyes drifted shut and she sighed dreamily.

"Such things you make me feel, Cutter Blackwell," she murmured with a smile.

He leaned back, finished the rest of the grapes, then stretched out his arms behind him, tipping his face to the sun, allowing the warmth to bathe his skin.

"It's beautiful here, you know that?" he said quietly, realizing he meant it. Since he'd arrived, he'd found a kind of peacefulness in this quiet little backward community.

Perhaps it was just that he'd lived and thrived on constant action and movement, he'd never taken the time to appreciate how quiet and peaceful life could be.

He turned to her, surprised to see her watching him. He glanced away, because looking at Sara made him want things he knew better than to want.

Now that the moment of truth had arrived, he was surprised at how quickly panic had risen. Not because of what he had to tell her, but because she would realize he'd deceived her. Lied to her. Deliberately.

And he didn't know how she'd take it.

Needing to do something with his hands, he sat up and began foraging in the basket again.

"Are you hungry, Cutter?" Sara asked, pulling

covered dishes out of the basket and setting them on the blanket.

The heavenly aromas had him digging under the lids. "God, this smells wonderful." His stomach grumbled loudly, making her laugh. "I didn't realize I was hungry until you got here."

He lifted his head. Their eyes caught, held, and he realized it wasn't just food he was hungry for, but for her, as well.

"Cutter." She whispered his name on a trembling breath, and her mouth parted into a small O.

He said a silent prayer for strength, then pushed the basket out of the way as he reached for her, needing to touch her.

He did.

Control slipped through his fingers, scattering somewhere in the spring breeze. "Sara." Nothing came out but her name as he crushed his mouth to hers, wanting to drown in the taste and feel of her.

Her mouth opened slowly, shyly, under his, and Cutter couldn't stop the groan that tore through him. His hands ran the length of her back, feeling the smooth, straight line of her spine, the gentle curve of her hips, the slender column of her neck, warmed from the veil of her freed hair.

"Sara." He murmured her name, struggling to hang on to the last bit of his self-control as she tugged him closer, pressing against him until his body was nearly vibrating with need and desire. "We can't...we...have...to stop."

"No, Cutter," she murmured back. "I do not want to stop." She drew away only enough to look at him, to trace his cheek with the tips of her fingers, her heart in her eyes. "Cutter, I love you—"

"No, Sara, you don't mean that, you can't—"

"Yes," she insisted firmly, pressing kisses to his face, clinging to him. "I do mean it, Cutter Blackwell. I have loved you almost from the moment we met. Something in my heart, in my woman's heart, recognized you as if I had known you my whole life, as if I had been waiting for you since the day I was born."

Her words set off a warning bell in his mind, a reminder that hit far too close to home, for he, too, had experienced that feeling of recognition the moment he'd laid eyes on her.

As if she had been what he'd been looking for, waiting for, his whole life.

His thoughts fragmented and his control quickly evaporated as she continued to press kisses to his face, his mouth, whispering against his lips.

"I love you, Cutter, and it is not wrong. Nothing that feels like this could be wrong. Not to me. Not to God."

He was trying to breathe, trying to hold on, but with every breath he could taste her sweetness, smell her innocence, and it was wreaking havoc with his senses.

"Cutter, I want you to make love with me."

Desire and need collided inside him, and all his good intentions wavered and began to retreat. He'd tried hard to keep her at bay, away from his heart, but somehow when he wasn't looking, she'd snuck in, claiming a spot for herself. And he never saw it coming.

"I love you, Cutter," she whispered, leaning against him until they were both sprawled flat on the blanket, their legs tangled together. "I know that I cannot have you, but I can have this with you. If this is all I can have, please let me. It is something I will cherish the rest of my life, knowing that the one man, the only man I have ever loved, will ever love, once loved me in return."

He heard the sadness, the plea, and it nearly broke his heart.

"Oh, Sara." He wrapped his arms tightly around her, holding her close, heart to heart, the ache inside him so deep he knew nothing could appease it but her.

Only Sara.

His Sara.

He fought for control, struggled to even his breathing. "We have...to talk." He couldn't let this happen, not until he told her the truth.

"No. Later. Much later, Cutter. Please?"

The soft, pleading word was his undoing. Sanity fled, evaporating like mist on a heated morning.

''Sara.'' Her name was a prayer as he pulled her fully atop him, his mouth claiming hers, his hands finally possessing what he thought he could never have.

He kneaded her flesh, slid his hands reverently down her back, her buttocks, to the top of her thighs. Her dress had risen when they'd tumbled to the ground, and now he felt her satiny skin beneath his hands.

Sara squirmed against him, unaware of what her movement was doing to him. When she felt the cool, gentle touch of his hands on the back of her thighs, her legs parted in a motion so natural she was barely aware of it.

She rubbed herself against him, wanting to ease the sudden ache that had enveloped her body. Her mouth clung to his as he tumbled them over until she was lying beneath him, his warm, hard length covering her.

Right.

It felt so right, she thought hazily, wanting to remember every feeling, every new sensation, so that she could keep it in her mind forever.

Her mouth was greedy, her body searching, seeking some relief from the constant ache that seemed to grow stronger and stronger with each passing moment.

She had no idea she could feel so many things—even colors; she could almost feel the colors of joy, of love, seeping into her heart, her consciousness.

Cutter's hands slowly, gently, slid over her, cupping the gentle mound of her breast, kneading the aching nipple until she was moaning, arching against him, pleading for more.

She needed to touch him. Skin to skin. She tugged at his shirt, freeing it from his jeans, running her hands up the long, sculptured back, reveling in the sheer warmth and masculinity of him.

It wasn't enough.

Frantic, she fumbled with the buttons, and he swore softly, expertly, as he tugged it over his head and tossed it aside to savage her mouth once again.

Her breath came out on a hushed gasp when she felt the warm spring air on her bare flesh. And Cutter's bare chest, warm and firm, pressing against her own.

Her apron, her dress, had come off easily, quickly, and panting softly, she clung to Cutter, drawing closer, wanting to touch him everywhere at once.

He took her breast in his mouth and suckled, and she cried out, clinging to him, arching upward, offering him more. Oh, how much she'd wanted this. These feelings of love and intimacy with the man she loved more than anything else in the world.

Cutter was struggling to slow down, to hold on to some vestige of sanity, of control, but it was impossible with that sweet, silky body wrapped invitingly around him, with Sara's hands, her mouth, touching him everywhere.

He was dying, he thought as his vision hazed. Dying. It had never, ever been like this with a woman. It wasn't just their physical selves that were connecting, but for the first time in his life, Cutter felt a joining of souls, a completeness that he'd never imagined possible.

She was writhing under him, soft little moans escaping that sweet mouth. When he slid his hand down to cup her, her eyes flew open, and she gasped his name. For an instant, time seemed suspended, and then she cried out, her eyes closing as she began the quick, hot ascent into heaven.

"Sara." Her name came out a breathless prayer. He knew she was innocent; he knew he had to be gentle. To take care.

But she was pulling him closer, wrapping her legs around him, drawing him in. "Please, Cutter. Don't stop." She touched his face. "I love you," she whispered.

It was his undoing. He tumbled past sanity and drove inside her. She was hot, wet and tight. And welcoming. So welcoming.

He leveled himself on his elbows, struggling with his own need for release and the more urgent need not to hurt her. Sweat pooled on his back, his body, mingling with hers. Her body was warm and fragrant with her scent. And his. It was the most erotic scent he'd ever experienced, and he knew he'd never forget it.

He'd never forget her.

Or this moment.

If he was a man who was capable of love, of trust, he would have said he loved her.

But he knew better. Knew he wasn't capable of such an emotion.

Except for family.

She arched beneath him and he groaned again.

"Don't move," he warned, letting his eyes close. His breath was panting out in short little gasps, and his heart was thundering like a runaway train.

She smiled, a woman's secret smile, and he groaned, lost inside her.

"Oh, Cutter," she breathed as he slowly, carefully, began to move. "It's…it's…wonderful." Her eyes closed and she held him tight, moving with him until he could feel her trembling and shuddering beneath him.

He began to move faster, instinct tugging at him as need and desire took over, obliterating his thoughts, his common sense, his reason.

She moved with him, arching higher and higher, her breath hitching, her hands damp and slick with sweat, clinging to his hips, urging him on, pulling him deeper.

"Oh, Cutter!" She tumbled over the edge into the sensuous oblivion of release, taking him with her.

Pleasure so deep, so dark, so intense it made him senseless came out of nowhere, and with a low roar, he emptied himself inside her.

"Sara? Are you all right?" Worried and drained, he'd rolled to his back to ease his weight off her. He'd looped his arm around her, keeping her close, not wanting the moment to end.

Cutter's eyes closed and he inhaled a long, deep breath. He needed just a moment to let the strength, the life, seep back into him.

He lifted his head and looked at her. "Sara?" Panicked, he saw the tears glittering in the corner of her eye. "Did I hurt you?" He ran his free hand over her gently, making certain she was still all right.

She caught his hand, and her mouth curved into a beautiful, wondrous smile. "I am fine, Cutter Blackwell." She brought his hand to her mouth for a kiss. "Perfect. It…it…was beautiful." She let out a happy sigh, curling her naked body against him. "I had no idea it was possible to feel so many wonderful things."

"Did I hurt you?" He knew she was innocent and he worried that he'd been too rough, too fast, too insensitive.

"No, you did not hurt me, Cutter." She paused a

moment. "What you did is make me feel like a woman."

Her words had his heart catching and he drew her closer, burying his face in her hair. "Oh, Sara."

"Do not regret this, Cutter Blackwell, please." She laid a hand on his chest. "Do not ever regret this. It is what I wanted. I love you, and if this is all I can ever have of you, so be it. It will be enough."

"No, Sara." He rolled to face her. The sun was going down now, the air cooling. Their bodies were damp with sweat, and he saw her shiver. He ran his hand up and down her arm, trying to keep her warm. "Sara, that's wrong. This shouldn't be all that you get from life. There is so much more."

He wanted her to know of the world beyond the settlement. A world where anything was possible: the fulfillment of dreams, the quenching of desire.

And love.

Unrestricted, uncomplicated love.

A man for a woman.

The kind of love that wasn't restricted to honor, respect and duty. The kind of love that flowed easily, comfortably, effortlessly, *endlessly,* from a man to a woman.

The kind of love his parents shared.

The kind of love he'd never believed possible until Sara.

"Ach, yes, I know there is more to life, Cutter." she laid her hand on his cheek. "Because of you, I know this now.'' Her lips curved into a gentle smile. ''And I will always be grateful to you for giving me this gift of knowledge, this gift of love. I will it treasure forever, deep in my heart.''

''Oh, Sara.'' How could he fight the feelings swamping him when she said things that tugged at his heart, a heart he wasn't even certain he still had.

Until he'd met her.

As if sensing he needed her strength and comfort now, Sara merely held him, letting her hands run the length of him. ''Do not feel sad, Cutter Blackwell,'' she whispered, her soft breath fanning his face. ''I love you, and I am not now nor will I ever be ashamed of what is in my heart.''

He held her tighter.

''You should rejoice. It is a joy to give someone such a rare and precious gift. And you have done this for me.'' She pressed a kiss to his cheek as he slid his leg over her, drawing her closer.

''And you've given me a rare and precious gift, Sara,'' he whispered, kissing her neck, savoring the scent he would always associate with her. ''One I will always treasure.''

With a smile, she looked at him curiously. ''And what is that, Cutter?''

''Your heart.''

A heart, he knew, he was about to break.

Chapter Eleven

It was dark by the time they'd finished their picnic dinner. Sated and satisfied, Cutter helped Sara clean up, then pack everything back in the basket.

He drew her to him, then leaned against the towering oak, glancing up at the sky.

"It's so peaceful out here, and so beautiful."

"It is a beautiful world, Cutter." She smiled up at him. "Especially my world, because you are in it."

The moment she said the words, he stiffened. "Sara, I need to talk to you," he said.

She sighed. "Yes, Cutter, I know. I know what you are going to say."

"You do?" he asked in surprise, his heart tripping into panic.

"Yes, Cutter. I know that you are leaving." Her voice had dropped to a whisper that had him drawing her closer.

"Is that what you think I wanted to talk to you about?"

"Is it not?" she asked, her gaze searching his.

"No, Sara," he began carefully, saying a silent prayer to a God he thought he'd stopped believing in years ago to give him a helping hand. "There's something else I have to tell you. Something more important."

"Cutter, nothing is more important than the fact of your leaving." Her voice was firm, like the schoolteacher she was and he struggled not to smile. His Sara was a study in contradictions.

Watching her, he took a breath, searched for the right words, then decided to just plunge in. "Sara, I'm not who you think I am."

"You are not the man I love?" she asked with a smile.

He shifted uncomfortably, more nervous than he believed possible. "I'm not...Endy's nephew."

She looked at him for a long moment. "I do not understand, Cutter."

He blew out a breath and dragged his free hand through his hair. "Sara, I'm not related to Endy at all. He's an old military contact I've known for a long time."

"And?" she prodded, sensing there was more.

"And I didn't come here to see Endy. I came to find you."

"Find me?" Her brows drew together. "But, Cutter, I was not lost and you did not even know me before you arrived at Endy's house." She shook her head. "I do not understand what you're saying."

"Sara, I did know you before we met, in a manner of speaking," he said, rushing on at the look on her face. "Remember I told you about my brothers, my adopted brothers?"

"Yes," she said slowly. "You have two adopted brothers, Colt and Hunter."

"Right, well, remember I told you that Colt had a younger brother who died in a fire?"

"Yes, of course, but—"

He cut her off, realizing if he didn't he might lose his nerve. "Well, Colt also had a younger sister, a sister he never knew about. She was born after Colt was adopted by the Blackwells. My adoptive mother just learned about this about eight months ago when she received a letter from Colt's mother." Blowing out another breath, Cutter stared into the darkness. he couldn't bear to watch Sara's face when she learned of his deception. "Colt's mother was dying, and I guess she figured she'd do one good thing for her children. She sent my mother a letter telling her that Colt had a sister, a child she'd given up when she was barely two. She didn't tell my mother any more, but my mother decided then and there to find Colt's sister. So she asked for my help.''

''And did you find Colt's sister?'' Sara asked, her heart pounding.

''Yes, Sara, I did.'' He reached for her, dropping his hands to her shoulders. ''Sara, you're Colt's sister.''

He watched the color drain from her face, watched the disbelief fill her eyes, followed quickly by tears of hurt, of confusion.

''What are you saying, Cutter?'' Her frantic gaze sought his.

''I spent six months tracking you down. Six months investigating, and then about a month ago, I learned that you had been adopted by an Amish family in southern Illinois. From there, it wasn't hard to do some digging to find out who in the settlement had an adopted daughter.''

Sara shook her head, unable to fathom what he was telling her. For her whole life she had yearned for this knowledge, but now that she had it, the joy was tainted by something far more powerful: pain at Cutter's deception.

''You knew...'' She had to swallow. ''You knew all along who I was? From when you first arrived?''

''Yes.''

''But...but why did you not tell me? Why...why did you keep this a secret from me?'' Her voice was catching in an effort not to cry. ''Why...why did you lie to me about who you were and why you were here?''

''I didn't intend to, Sara, but I had to be sure, and I wanted a chance to get to know you so I could figure out the best way to tell you.''

''You lied to me, Cutter Blackwell. From the beginning, you lied.'' The tears came, and she couldn't control them. The enormity of what he'd told her had her emotions rushing headlong, crashing into one another, breaking her heart. ''You pretended to be my friend. You said I could trust you. And I did trust you.''

She had loved him and trusted him as she had no other.

''Sara.'' He held her tight, forcing her to look at him. ''You can trust me, Sara. You have trusted me,'' he added quietly. ''With your heart. I didn't lie to you about anything else except who I was and why I was here. You have to believe me, Sara. You have to.''

She sniffled, swiping at her eyes. ''Believe you,'' she said quietly. ''How can I believe you, Cutter, when I gave you my love, my heart, and you gave me back...lies?''

''No, Sara, it wasn't like that. Please, you have to understand.''

''I do not understand any of this, Cutter.'' All she understood was that her heart was shattering like a fragile handblown glass. She pulled away from him, but he caught her hands.

"Sara." He went to touch her face, but she shied away from him. "Please, don't let my actions taint this news that I've brought you." He squeezed her hands. "You have a right to know your family. Your brother, your real brother. We want you to come to Texas, to meet Colt. To have a chance to do what you've always yearned to do, to finally know who you really are."

"Texas." She pressed a hand to her head. It was spinning, making it difficult for her to think. How could he give her so much with one hand and take so much with the other. "You want me to come to Texas?" She could imagine flying to the moon just as readily. Shaking her head, she laughed, but the sound was hauntingly sad. "I am sorry, Cutter, but in case you have forgotten, I do not have the money to fly across the world."

"Country," he amended gently. "Texas is in this country." He fished in his pocket and pulled something out, pressing it into her hand. "Take this."

She glanced down at the frayed handkerchief. Slowly, she opened it. Inside was a wad of dirty, wrinkled bills. "What is this about, Cutter Blackwell?" She looked up at him. "More tricks?"

"No," he said. "It's freedom, Sara. It's just pocket money, Sara, so you'll have some cash on you. All your expenses will be paid by my family. You'll find our address in there, as well.''

"Your...your brother—"

"*Your* brother," he corrected. "Colt wants to meet you."

"How...how do you know this?" She had to fight back the pain in her heart, to concentrate on what he was telling her.

"Because my parents flew up from Florida last week to tell Colt where I was and that he had a sister. They told him I was going to try to convince you to come to Texas to meet him."

"And what did your—Colt—" She said his name firmly, unable to say *my brother* yet. It was too new, too scary "—say?"

"Hurry up."

Her gaze flew to his. "Excuse me, please?"

"Colt said you should hurry up. He can't wait to meet you, Sara."

"My brother," she whispered reverently, clutching the handkerchief to her chest. She wouldn't let the tears come, not now. Not in front of Cutter. This was too personal, too private, something she'd yearned for in her heart for so long that now that it had happened, it almost seemed too miraculous to comprehend.

She had a brother.

A real brother.

A family.

"He—"

"Colt, Sara, his name is Colt."

She swallowed. "Colt...he is English like you?"

"Yes, Sara, he's English like me."

She nodded. "Then I, too, was English?"

"Yes, Sara. You *are* English," Cutter said. "I never meant to hurt you, Sara." He touched her cheek. "You have to believe me."

"I do not know what to believe, Cutter Blackwell." She squeezed her eyes shut, feeling as if there wasn't enough air in the world any longer. "I just do not know what to believe."

"Believe that I never meant to hurt you." He reached for her hands again. "Please, Sara, say you believe me and that you'll come to Texas."

"No, Cutter, I will not say that." She pressed a hand to her forehead where a pain had started. "I...I need to think."

She'd been born English.

Now she understood why she'd never fitted in, why she'd always felt different, unworthy, unable to conform or comprehend all the rigid rules that had guided her life.

She'd been born English.

And she had a brother.

The knowledge sent a secret thrill of hope through her, but that hope was tinged with an almost unbearable sadness.

Sara stood up. "I must go now, Cutter."

He rose, as well. "Go? Where are you going?"

''Back to Endy's. I need to think, Cutter, and I cannot do it here.''

''Sara.'' He bent and reached for the supper basket, handing it to her. ''Please, say that you forgive me.''

She lifted her head and looked at him, her eyes glittering with fresh tears. ''No, Cutter Blackwell, I am sorry, I cannot say I forgive you.'' Her aching heart softened at the look of devastation on his face. ''Not yet,'' she whispered, turning away from him.

She was gone in the morning when he woke up.

''Left about dawn,'' Endy informed him when he came tearing downstairs looking for her. ''Said to tell you that you should go home. Back to Texas.''

Cutter's heart felt as if someone had stepped on it. ''Did she say anything else?''

''Nope.'' Endy rubbed his stubbled chin. ''Only that she needed some time to think.''

''Endy, what the hell should I do?''

Endy patted his shoulder. ''Go home.'' He smiled. ''And wait.''

He waited three days, but he didn't hear from her, and so, he left with no choice, feeling miserable and heartsick, Cutter flew home, knowing that he'd broken the heart of the only woman he'd ever loved.

Sara was miserable. And torn.

For two weeks she tried to muddle through the

days, but at night, her memories of Cutter and their lovemaking, her love for him, haunted her.

As did the knowledge that her brother was waiting for her—in Texas—and she did not know what to do.

One night at dinner, the decision came quickly and with such clarity that Sara wondered why it had been so difficult to make.

"I've invited Joshua to Sunday supper," her father said, not bothering to look at her. "I've given him permission to take you riding."

Sara pushed her plate away, her food untouched. "No, Papa, I'm sorry, but I cannot go riding with Joshua on Sunday."

The stillness that followed her announcement reverberated through the room like a cannon shot. She had never once spoken back or openly defied her father before. It was not done.

Her father's head lifted, his face thunderous. "What is it you say, daughter?"

Sara glanced at her mother, who looked frightened and fragile and was wringing her hands because of her daughter's defiance.

Her gaze shifted to her little brother, Josef, precious Josef, whose eyes had widened into saucers.

Her love for them was deep, but Sara knew this was something she had to do, but she would try to do it in the easiest way possible. She had no wish to hurt them.

Her chin lifted. "Papa, I cannot go riding with Joshua and I cannot pretend to want to."

"It is not for you to decide, daughter." Furious that she so brazenly opposed him, her father pushed his chair from the table, then stormed out the back door.

"Give him a moment, Sara," her mother said, reaching across the table to pat her hand. "He just wants your happiness, that is all."

As long as it conformed to what he thought would make her happy, Sara thought bitterly, standing up. "I will go speak to him." Grabbing her shawl off the peg, Sara hurried after her father, knowing she'd find him in the barn.

"Papa."

"Did you come to disrespect your father out here, as well?"

"No, Papa." She moved closer to him, wishing she could reach out to him, to touch him, to really reach him so that he could see what was in her heart—her torn heart. A heart torn between her love and gratitude toward him and her mother for what they'd done for her, given her, and torn between finally knowing who she really was, and her real family.

She wanted to reach him to let him know this, but she also wanted to reach him so that he could perhaps try to understand how important this was to her. More important than anything she'd ever done.

"I came out here to tell you something." She moved closer. "I am going to Texas."

For a moment, it was as if her words did not register. Her father stared at her, and then it seemed as if the strength, the life, drained out of him. He sat down heavily on the small milking stool.

"What is this?" His eyes narrowed suspiciously. "What kind of shame will you bring to this family now?"

"I bring no shame to you, Papa." She took a deep breath. "Do you remember the man who came to stay at Mr. Enderly's?"

"His nephew?" He nodded, his expression wary. "I remember. The man I told you to stay away from."

"Yes, Papa," she said, trying not to feel shame. "He was not Endy's nephew." Nervous, Sara licked her lips. "He came here to find me. He had news of my family. My brother. My real brother." Her father said nothing, only frowned at her. "My brother lives in Texas, and...and I am going there to meet him."

"You will go nowhere," he thundered. "Do you hear me?"

"I am going, Papa," she said quietly, her determination strong. "This is something I must do. I tell you out of respect for you and love for you."

"You do not respect your family, your faith. You have let this...this English fill your mind with worldly ideas. No good will come of this, mark my words."

"I am going, Papa," she repeated sadly, letting her tears slip unheeded down her cheeks. "This I must do. I pray that someday you will understand.'' Sara turned and walked out of the barn, her steps faltering, trying not to cry.

''If you go, daughter, you will not come back here.''

She squeezed her eyes shut against the pain of his words and kept on walking away from the only world, the only family, she had ever known.

Chapter Twelve

"Sara honey, you all right?" Endy stood in the doorway of her bedroom, a worried look on his face. "The taxi to take us to the airport will be here in less than an hour."

"I'm fine," she said with a false brightness she didn't feel. Her stomach felt as if it were tied in tight knots and getting tighter every moment. "I'm just finishing the last of my packing."

"I'll wait for you downstairs, then." Endy started to say something else, then seemingly deciding it was best left unsaid, started back downstairs again.

When Sara had arrived at his doorstep three nights ago, her face pale and streaked with tears, he'd taken her into the house, into his arms.

"Shh, don't cry, honey, everything will be fine," he had told her as he rocked her. She had been emotionally drained and exhausted; the toll of leaving her family, losing Cutter, learning of his deception, showed clearly on her face.

Gently, he'd led her up to her bedroom, then sat with her until she'd cried herself to sleep.

In the days since, he'd helped her address a letter to her brother Colt, telling him she was coming to Texas to meet him.

He'd made arrangements for a taxi to take them to the airport and let her brother Josef come over every afternoon to see her. Each day, poor little Josef struggled with a box of Sara's things, and each day when Sara saw her little brother, she cried.

Now, they were scheduled to leave in less than an hour, and as their departure drew closer, Sara grew more pale, more nervous.

The doorbell rang just as Endy reached the bottom step. When he went to answer it, he saw Sara's father standing in the doorway.

"I would like to see my daughter, please." Clutching his hat nervously in his hands, Josef Gunter stared directly into Endy's curious eyes.

"Come on in, Mr. Gunter. She's right upstairs." He ushered Sara's father into the foyer. "I'll go get her."

Endy bounded up the stairs with a gait that defied

his age, nearly skidding to a halt outside Sara's bedroom.

"Got a visitor, Sara." He went into the room and took her by the hand, nearly dragging her toward the door. "Your father is here. He wants to see you."

"My father," she said in a panic, hanging back. "What does he want?"

"I'm sure I don't know. And you won't know, either, unless you go downstairs and see him."

"I...I don't know if I can see him," she admitted. She'd forced herself to say a final, painful farewell to the only family she had ever known. Hadn't her father told her if she went to Texas, she couldn't come back?

So what was he doing here now? Did he want to rub salt into her aching, pain-filled wounds?

"Sara, honey," Endy said with a sigh, "you got to see him. He's your father." He gave her a little push to get her moving. "And make it quick. Our taxi will be here soon," he said, watching her head toward the stairs.

Josef was standing in the foyer, clutching his hat in his hands. He glanced up as Sara came down the stairs.

"Papa," she said as she faced him, lifting her chin and steeling herself for anything. "You wanted to speak to me?"

He looked at her carefully. "So you are going to Texas, then?"

"Yes, Papa."

He nodded solemnly. "I have something for your journey, Sara." He paused to dip in the pocket of his black broadcloth pants.

Sara blinked at him in surprise. He had never, ever addressed her by her given name; he had always called her daughter.

"Something for my journey?" she asked in confusion.

He pulled out a small brown leather pouch with a single drawstring. He held it out to her.

"What is this, Papa?" she asked, taking the pouch.

He glanced down at the toes of his black work boots. "It...it...is the money you have earned while you have worked here." He glanced around. "In this house." He took a deep breath, and it seemed to shudder out of him. "I...I was saving it for the lumber to buy your marital house. So that you would have something to start your new life with." His fingers tightened on his hat, nearly crushing the brim. "But I think you need it now to start your new life." She could hear the pain in his voice and knew how much it cost him to come here, to do this for her.

"Oh, Papa." As she stood there clutching the pouch to her heart, Sara's eyes flooded with tears. "Thank you, Papa. Thank you."

She knew how much the family needed the extra money, which was one of the reasons she had taken the job with Endy. She had no idea he had saved every penny for her. It touched her deeply.

Twisting his hat between nervous fingers, Josef glanced down at his heavy work boots again. "I have...I have always been hard on you."

Her throat closed at his confession. "Yes, Papa."

"You thought it was because I did not love you. Or because I did not think you worthy." He shook his head. "This was not so, Sara." He took a deep breath, and she could see the trembling of his lips.

"Papa?" Worried, she took a step closer, laying a hand on his chest, wanting to ease his pain.

"No." He held up his large hand. It, too, was trembling. "Please. Let me finish." Taking a deep breath, Josef continued. "It was because I loved you so, daughter, that I was so hard on you." He finally looked at her and she could see tears glistening in his eyes. "Even though you were not born of my blood, daughter, you were born of my heart." He laid one of his large, work-roughened hands on his chest. "In here, you were always my precious daughter." He had to swallow before continuing. "I always feared that someday your—family—"

"You are my family, Papa," she insisted, unable to bear seeing him like this.

He shook his head, unable to speak for a moment. Sara watched as he swallowed hard several times. He opened his mouth, but no words came out as he seemed to struggle to maintain control.

Finally, he took a deep breath and went on. "No, Sara. God only gave you to us for a little while. I understand that. I have always understood that, and perhaps I thought if I was hard on you, if I made you love our life, then when the day came and your birth family—" His voice broke.

"Papa, please, no. This is not necessary."

"Yes," he said, his voice filled with emotion. "It is necessary. I thought that if I made you love our life, then you would never leave us." He shook his head. "I was trying to outguess God," he said sadly. "It is God's will that your family—your birth family—has found you, and God's will that you must go to them." His head bobbed slowly, as if giving her permission for all she held in her heart. "I understand this, daughter. But I did not want you to leave thinking that I...I did not love you."

He reached for her hand and held it tightly between his two big ones, crushing his hatband in the process.

"I love you, daughter." Unashamed tears swam in his eyes. "I have always loved you. So much. I...I was afraid to face this day." Sniffling, he released one of her hands to reach for his handkerchief and blow his nose. "But I was selfish, daughter—*Hochmut*. It was a sin for me to fear this. A sin to try to stop you from obeying God's will. I am a man of deep faith and I am...ashamed."

"No, Papa." Sobbing, Sara went to her father, the only father she had ever known, and threw her arms around him, hugging him for the first time in her life. "You were not selfish. I understand."

Awkwardly, he patted her back. "Ahh, see such a good daughter you are, excusing your father's sins," he said. "May I ask a favor, daughter?" he asked, looking down at her from what she always thought was an imperial height.

Sara snuffled. "Anything, Papa. Anything."

"Will you...will you come back to see us?" He blew his nose again. "I ask only because your mother and baby brother...they will miss you so—"

"Oh, Papa," she said, hugging him tighter, burying her face in his broad barrel chest, feeling a safety and comfort that only a father can give.

She knew what he was trying to tell her. That he would miss her. Her heart, which had always seemed so empty, suddenly seemed full to overflowing.

"I would like to come back," she admitted, swiping at her eyes, wanting no tears.

Her father drew back to look at her. "My beautiful daughter."

Her throat closed so tightly it was an effort to breathe, to speak. "Papa, I—"

He shook his head. "No, Sara, I want you to go, to meet your brother, to see what your life would have been like. It was God's will. I have already gone to speak to the deacons. They, too, understand God's will. They understand this is something you must do. But if you want to come back to us, you are always welcome. They have said you can still teach at the settlement school if you like.''

Her heart soared. She knew the consequences of her actions might have prevented her from teaching in the settlement again. But her father's words soothed the worry that had been a painful ache in her heart.

"Sara. Daughter.'' He grabbed her close again, stroking a hand gently down her *kapp*. "You are always welcome to come back and you will always be wanted, daughter.'' He hugged her tighter. "I love you, Sara,'' he whispered softly. "I love you. Remember that you are always welcome to return to your family.''

Sniffling, she clung to him for a long moment, then stepped back. "Thank you, Papa.'' The little leather pouch was still clutched—crushed—in her fist. "And thank you for this.'' She held it up. "But I don't need it. I have—''

"Ach, no.'' Alarmed, he shook his head. "You are not used to traveling in the English world. I hear it is a very costly world, and I want you to have all that you need.'' He glanced away. "I wish I could give you more.''

"No, Papa.'' She shook her head, wiped away her tears. "You have given me the best gift of all. Your love, and my family.'' Standing on tiptoe, she kissed his cheek. "That is all that I need.''

He nodded, glancing around behind him at the sound of a blaring horn.

"Sara, honey," Endy said gently, coming into the foyer with their bags, "the taxi's here to take us to the airport." Skirting around them, Endy opened the door and started carrying their bags toward the waiting cab.

"Papa—"

"No." He held up his hand. "You must do this, Sara." He fiddled with his hatband before settling his hat firmly and comfortably atop his head. "We will accept whatever happens, daughter." He shrugged, trying to smile. "Even I am not so bold as to think that I can change or alter God's will. So old and feeble I am not." He stopped to look at her for a moment. Then he stepped closer, cradling her face in his large hands. "You are loved, daughter. Always remember that."

"I will." She didn't think it was possible for her heart to break in two a second time.

He bent and kissed both of her cheeks, pausing to swipe a tear away with his thumb. "You will be much missed."

"I'll miss you, too, Papa."

"Safe journey, then."

"Thank you, Papa." She wanted to cling to him, to curl up in his arms and stay, but she knew she couldn't. She had to go to Texas to meet her brother and to settle this matter with Cutter.

But she would go now with her heart full and her conscience clear, for she knew that what she was doing was God's will.

So how could she do less?

"I will bid farewell to your mother and brother for you."

"Thank you."

He seemed reluctant to leave. "Good day to you, Sara."

She smiled, noting that he did not say the traditional goodbye. "Good day to you, Papa."

With a nod and a smile, he turned and walked out the door, leaving Sara smiling after him.

Blackwell, Texas

"What time is it now?" Colt asked, swiveling around on the kitchen stool and earning a swat on the back of his head from Cutter.

"About thirty seconds later than the last time you asked."

Cutter glanced at the kitchen clock. Again. Sara was arriving today. In less than an hour, he figured, glancing at his watch to check the time again. He didn't know who was more nervous, Colt or him.

He'd been dying inside, dying with need and loneliness. He couldn't sleep, couldn't eat; all he could do was think of her.

And how he'd hurt her.

He hadn't been able to forget the sight of her tear-streaked face; the shock in her eyes when she'd learned of his deception. And he didn't know if he'd be able to forgive himself for what he'd done to her. He wasn't certain he deserved to be forgiven.

When Sara's letter arrived addressed to Colt, informing him that she was coming to Texas, Cutter's heart soared, but she'd made no mention of him in the letter, and so now he, just like Colt, waited.

Although for entirely different reasons.

Pacing the long length of the kitchen, Cutter paused to pour himself a cup of coffee from the ever-present pot.

Always intuitive, his mother had shanghaied everyone else in the family out of the house for the afternoon so that Sara wouldn't feel overwhelmed, and so that Colt and Sara would have some time to spend alone. Cutter had to admit he was looking forward to spending some time alone with Sara, as well.

"Is that a car?" Colt jumped from the stool, and Baby, the mongrel dog they'd adopted years ago, who was the size of a small pony, merely lifted her head, yawned in boredom, then laid her head down on her paws and went back to sleep.

Cutter sighed. "No, Colt, that wasn't a car." He gently nudged the dog with the toe of his boot. "If it was a car, Baby would be up barking, howling and running laps around the table."

Colt turned to scowl at the dog. "Lazy beast," he said affectionately.

Digging into his pocket, Colt pulled out Sara's letter and reread it for perhaps the hundredth time. Cutter could see that the pages were now wrinkled and nearly worn through in spots.

"Uh, Cutter, can I ask you something, bro?"

"No."

"What…what should I say to her?"

"You, the man with the golden tongue when it comes to women, are asking me what you should say?" Shaking his head, Cutter chuckled.

"Yeah, but this is different, Cutter. This is my…sister. I mean, when I first lay eyes on her, I'm not sure what the right approach is." Blowing out a nervous breath, Colt sighed. "I've gone over in my mind a hundred different things to say, but I just can't figure out exactly what's the right thing."

"Colt?"

"What, Cutter?"

Cutter nodded toward the front door. "*That* was a car."

Colt jumped to his feet, nearly knocking over the stool. Alerted, Baby jumped up and started howling, then began racing around the kitchen table, barking loudly, her nails clicking against the marble floor, nearly knocking Colt and Cutter down in the process.

"Down, girl," Cutter growled, pointing a finger at

Baby as Colt headed toward the front door. "Stay down."

The dog obeyed and, satisfied she wouldn't scare Sara out of her sensible shoes, Cutter followed Colt to the open front door.

"That's Endy," Cutter said as the older man got out of the cab parked in the driveway.

Endy reached in a hand to help Sara, and slowly, shyly, she emerged from the cab, blinking against the harsh Texas sun, her eyes widening at the sight of the house and its surroundings.

"And that's Sara," Cutter said softly, pushing open the screen door for Colt.

Mesmerized, Colt let his eyes drink her in. He felt something he hadn't felt in years: recognition. Even from this distance, he could see the resemblance. She was part of him and part of Cade, their late brother. She had the same dark hair, the same blue eyes. She was one of them.

His sister.

A fist squeezed his heart and Colt realized he shouldn't have worried about what he was going to say because he simply couldn't speak.

He could only stare.

Sara stood transfixed in the driveway, unable to do little more than stare herself at the man standing on the porch. She did not need a formal introduction. She would have known this man anywhere; her heart would have recognized him even if her eyes did not.

This…this was her brother.

Colt.

Her family.

Her heart seemed to stop and she pressed a hand to her mouth, stifling the sobs that were threatening to break loose.

In the end, Colt said nothing. He bolted down the porch, sprinted across the driveway and, with a war cry, lifted Sara off her feet and twirled her around in his arms, holding her close, letting her settle comfortably, irrevocably, into his empty heart.

"Brother," she whispered through her tears, stroking a hand down the sleek cap of black hair so like her own. "Dearest brother." Wrapping her arms around him, Sara buried her face in his shoulder and cried.

"Welcome home, baby sister," Colt whispered through his own tears. "Welcome home."

"So what will you do now, Sara?" Colt asked after she'd been there over a week. They were sitting on the front porch, on the Blackwell family swing, and she couldn't help but think about the night she and Cutter had sat on a similar swing. It seemed like a million years ago, she thought sadly.

The week since she'd arrived had gone by so quickly. As if time had wings. She'd spent almost all that time with Colt although Cutter was around enough for her to occasionally catch a glimpse of him.

She knew what he was doing and she loved him even more for it. He was trying to give her the opportunity to know her brother. A week to make up for all the lost years.

Even though her heart was still aching at Cutter's deception, Sara knew that, no matter what, she would never, ever stop loving Cutter. But she knew they had no future. He was home now, and soon, she thought, perhaps she would return home, as well.

She wished there were some way for her to live two lives: one in Illinois in the settlement so she could be with her family. And another life here, in Texas, with Cutter and her brother Colt.

Two families, two homes.

One love.

Cutter.

Sara sighed. But she knew such a fantasy was just foolishness. She knew before she fell hopelessly in love with Cutter that there was no way they could share a life together.

She couldn't live in his world.

He couldn't live in hers.

"Sara?" Colt prompted, watching her.

"What?" She blinked, realizing she had been daydreaming, then she smiled. "I am sorry, Colt." She laid a hand on his arm. "What was it that you asked?"

"What you're going to do now." She'd planned on spending two weeks with him, but now the first week was well over. It was a week they'd spent getting to know one another. A week he'd spent catching her up on his life before and after the Blackwells had adopted him.

He couldn't speak to her about Cade, the little brother they'd lost in the fire that had nearly taken Colt's life, as well. Even after all these years he still couldn't speak about it with anyone.

"I do not know for sure," Sara replied with a sigh, tipping her head back to look at the glorious stars glimmering in the black Texas sky.

"Are you planning on putting my brother out of his misery?" he asked with a smile. He'd have to be unconscious not to see that whatever had happened between Sara and Cutter in Illinois was not only incredibly powerful, but apparently not over.

Or resolved.

He owed his brother big time. More importantly, he loved him. And he had come to love his sister Sara. He wanted them both to be happy, and it was clear that they could only be happy together.

Clear, he supposed, to everyone but *them*.

"Misery?" Sara blinked at Colt. "I do not understand this phrase, Colt," she admitted, then she smiled at the look on his face. "So this 'putting my brother out of his misery' is another one of your teasings, is it not?"

Colt laughed, loving her quaint way of talking. Loving every single thing about her. He reached for her hand and tugged her close, wanting to smother a lifetime's worth of affection on her in the short time they had together. "Yep. It's my teasing again."

Laughing, she nodded. "And are you going to explain this teasing phrase to me? Or leave me to guess what it means?"

He pretended to consider for a moment. "I think I'll leave you guessing."

"Oh, you." Grinning, she reached for his ear and gave it a playful tug, the way she would her brother Josef when he was mischievous.

Colt gave a yelp that had Baby lifting her head, opening one eye, then promptly snuggling back down to sleep after deciding Colt was on his own.

"It means, Sara, that Cutter is miserable."

"And why do you say this, Colt?" she asked, suddenly worried. She had not spoken to her brother about her love for Cutter or about his deception.

Such a thing was far too private; she wanted to hold the memory of Cutter's love in her heart. And she wanted to forget the deception that had broken it. She was having a difficult time doing either.

"Have you gotten a good look at him lately?"

"Yes," she admitted slowly. "I...I look at him all the time. Whenever he is around." Realizing what she'd just said, she blushed, making Colt grin.

He didn't realize women did that anymore. He found it—and everything about Sara—absolutely delightful. "I know. That's why I'm asking if you're going to put him out of his misery." He knew from the look on her face she didn't have a clue as to what he was talking about. "My brother, in case you haven't noticed, is in love with you."

She stared at him mutely for a moment, then she shook her head firmly. "Ach, no, Colt. You are mistaken."

"Afraid not," Colt said confidently. "I've known him almost my whole life, and I've never seen him look or act this way, especially around or about a woman."

Colt knew that Cutter had had to deceive Sara in order to get close enough to her so that he could tell her who he really was. He did it in order to bring them together, something Colt appreciated more than he could ever express. So the least he could do was try to put things right with Sara.

Now that he'd gotten to know her, realized how truly innocent and loving she was, he could understand why she'd be devastated by Cutter's deception. And why his brother had fallen head over heels in love with her. Even if he'd yet to admit it. Maybe even to himself.

"You know," he said quietly, serious for one of the few times in his life, "if it wasn't for Cutter, you and I wouldn't be sitting here together right now."

"I know, and I am very grateful," she acknowledged. "But still, he deliberately deceived me." She sighed, the pain arcing through her. "That is not an easy thing to forget."

It was the culmination of all the things she'd always heard about the English, but then, when she thought of Cutter, she realized he was nothing like what she'd expected. He was kind, gentle, loving and considerate.

"Yeah, I can understand that. But it wasn't as if his intentions were dishonorable. He did it out of concern for you, because he cares about you, not because he was trying to hurt you."

"Is this what you truly believe, Colt?" she asked, unsure. She trusted this brother of hers from the depths of her soul. Not by the time they had known each other, but by what was in their hearts.

"You bet. I know Cutter almost as well as I know myself, and you'll never find a more honorable man. He's disgustingly honorable," Colt admitted with a scowl.

"This is not something that is disgusting, Colt," she scolded gently. "Honor is a good thing."

"Yeah, I know, Sara. That's what I'm trying to get you to see." Colt shifted his weight, pushing his foot against the porch floor to set the swing moving. "How would you have felt if Cutter had simply popped in to see you and dropped this little bombshell on you out of the blue, then walked away?"

She'd never thought of that before. "I do not

know," she answered honestly, realizing it probably would have been a much greater shock than it was.

"Exactly. I mean, think how shocking this could have been, this kind of news coming from an absolute stranger. You might not have even believed him. So it was probably a good thing that Cutter got to know you, become friends with you, so that he could break this news to you in a way that didn't frighten or alarm you."

Considering his words, Sara realized her brother had a point. "I see what you mean, Colt. It would not have been easy to believe such news from a total stranger, especially an—"

"English stranger," he finished for her with a smile. "You know, Sara, I don't know how to break this to you, but you're English, as well."

"I know," she said with a smile, realizing all the possibilities that came with the knowledge. "But I am also Amish." How could one person be two things, yet true and honorable to both? She did not know if such a thing was even possible.

Colt tilted his head to look at her. "So what do you think the chances are that an English man would've been able to get close enough to you in the settlement to tell you about me if Cutter hadn't deceived you?" He laughed. "From what you've told me about your life, it's not like he could just waltz up to the front door and make his announcement."

"Waltz?" She frowned. "What is this waltz?" she

asked, wanting to learn and understand every teasing phrase her brother used.

Colt laughed. "It's a dance, Sara."

"We are not allowed to dance," she said seriously. "And if Cutter had done this dance up to my front door, my father and the other men of the settlement would have been very alarmed."

Smiling, Colt shook his head, trying to remember she had a tendency to take everything he said literally. "No, Sara. 'Waltz up to the door' is just an expression."

Her eyes gleamed in amusement. "In this, you and Cutter are the same. Using expressions that make no sense."

Colt laughed again. "I guess you're right there. But you can see my point. If Cutter did just waltz—walk up to your front door and drop this news on you, how do you think you would have received it?"

It was her turn to laugh. "I would have thought he was just another crazy-in-the-head English man."

"Exactly. So now can you understand why Cutter did what he did? It wasn't to hurt you, Sara. No one wanted to hurt you. All Cutter wanted to do was re-unite me with a sister I never knew I had." Colt reached for her hand, lacing his fingers through hers. "And I'm glad he did."

"So am I," Sara said with a contented sigh, her mind going over what Colt had said. "So am I."

He was forcing her to think of things she had not

even considered before. All she had thought of was her own pain, her own broken heart and shattered trust.

"Do you love him?" Colt asked quietly.

"Ach, yes," she admitted soulfully, her eyes sliding shut. "As I have never loved another. Will ever love another."

"He loves you, too, Sara."

She turned to him, trying not to let hope flare. "And why do you say this, Colt?" she asked with a frown. "He has never expressed such a thing to me."

"Trust me on this, Sara—"

"Oh, I do trust you, Colt. Very much."

"Then trust this. Cutter loves you more than anything."

Sadness slipped over her like a veil. "Yes, Colt, but even is what you say is true, he has never expressed such a thing to me, and even if he did love me, the situation is…it is…hopeless. He cannot live in my world, and I cannot live in his."

"Cutter wouldn't tell you, Sara, because he wouldn't want you to feel as if you have to choose between him and the Gunters. Cutter wouldn't ever want to force you to make that kind of choice."

"So then it is hopeless, Colt." Sighing, she laid her head on his shoulder.

"Not necessarily." Colt grinned. "Where there's a will, there's a way."

Sara's brow arched at his words. "Another nonsense phrase, Colt?"

"Nope, this time I'm making a great deal of sense." Laughing, he set the swing in motion and told her his plan.

Three days passed before Sara had a chance to speak to Cutter alone. Either Emma or Justin or Sadie or Hunter or Colt would be around, and she had no opportunity to pull him aside.

She had no experience at this. No idea at all how to speak to a man about his feelings.

And so she worried for all three days, wanting to be prepared, going over the words in her mind so that she would not appear ignorant about such worldly things.

Finally, an opportunity arose one afternoon when everyone had scattered to purchase supplies for a party the Blackwells were having on the weekend.

Sadie, the Blackwell family housekeeper, the woman she had at one time jealously thought was Cutter's wife, had not only taken her under her wing, sharing recipes and teaching her to cook some new things, but Sadie had taken Endy under her wing, as well, although with a great deal more protest.

While everyone shopped in preparation for the party, she chose to stay home. Riding in motor cars made her stomach sway, and she wasn't crazy about the sensation.

She knew Cutter was home, as well, since he was helping his other brother, Hunter, mend some fences that ran along the back of the ranch. With Colt's words reverberating in her mind, Sara decided the time had come to talk to Cutter.

She had been passive her whole life simply because that was the way she'd been brought up. But about Cutter, she could never be passive.

She loved him too much.

And she could bear the ache in her heart no longer.

If he loved her, she needed to know.

Now.

But she had no experience in matters of men or love. No idea how she would go about finding out whether Cutter did indeed love her as Colt had said.

She had only three days left, three days before she went back to Illinois. To the only life she had ever known, without the only man she'd ever loved.

She had to take a chance to see if perhaps Colt was right. What did she have to lose when she'd lost Cutter already? He was worth taking a risk for; worth anything for what was in her heart.

The sun was hot and harsh, beating down on her as she picked her way across the expansive Blackwell land. With Cutter in sight, she found her heart in her throat and said a silent prayer she would find the right words to say what was in her heart in order to find out what was in his.

Dressed in worn jeans, he was stripped to the waist, sweating and swearing over a piece of ragged fence.

He heart lifted at the sight of him, at the body she loved and had loved. And that had loved her in return.

"You should not swear, Cutter," she said softly, startling him from behind.

He swore again and jumped, taken aback to find her standing behind him.

"Sara." Taking a deep breath, he dragged a hand through his hair. "You scared the life out of me."

Smiling, she couldn't resist, she laid a hand on his bare chest and felt the steady rhythm of his heart. "Not all the life, Cutter Blackwell. I can still hear your heart beating."

It wasn't beating, it was pounding like wildfire at the sight of her, at her touch.

It had never been like this with another woman.

Only Sara.

His Sara.

The only woman he would ever love; the only woman he couldn't have.

His heart contracted painfully as his gaze met hers, and he glanced away, unable to bear looking at her, unable to bear her touch, knowing he couldn't touch her, love her in return.

She was goodness, innocence, all the things he'd forgotten even existed in this world.

He'd seen too much of the world.

She hadn't seen enough.

He saw the world through cynical wary eyes.

She saw the world through the innocence of her inexperience.

It didn't matter.

He knew he loved her. Would always love her.

But he also knew he couldn't have her.

"What are you doing here?" he asked, his voice surly as he pulled off a work glove and mopped his brow.

"I came to ask you a question." Lacing her fingers together in front of her, with that serene smile, he thought she resembled exactly what she was: a prim and proper schoolteacher. He couldn't have loved anyone more.

"What question is that?" he asked curiously. She had a look about her, like a cat who'd swallowed a canary. It would have amused him if he wasn't struggling to hold on to his self-control, not to mention his sanity.

For almost two weeks he'd held back, kept his distance, not wanting to crowd her, wanting to give her the opportunity to get what she had yearned for her whole life without complicating that life for her.

She had a right to this time with Colt, a right to know her brother, her heritage, her people. Just as he had once yearned to know.

But he was dying inside.

Dying with his need for her; his love for her.

He didn't know how long he could maintain his

control. It was as slippery as a hot buttered knife. He wanted to haul her into her into her arms and kiss her, love her, just…love her.

But he knew it could never be.

His world.

Her world.

Never the twain shall meet.

"Do you love me, Cutter Blackwell?"

Innocent eyes, wide with hope, wide with love, stared into his, and Cutter found to his surprise he had to swallow hard against the rising tide of emotion.

"Do I *what?*" he asked, stalling against the frantic need that clawed at him.

"Love me?" she repeated, tipping her head to look into his clouded eyes. "Do you love me, Cutter Blackwell?"

The panic was swift and consuming. "What does that have to do with anything, Sara?" Blowing out a breath, he jammed a hand through his hair. "It doesn't matter one whit. You can't live in my world. I can't live in your world. You're Amish. I'm English." His voice was harsh with pain, with regret. "I'm adopted, too, Sara, remember? I would never want to have to choose between my adoptive family and the person I loved. Never. I couldn't. And I would never ask you to choose, either. And obviously you can't have both. So the matter is settled."

He turned from her, but the touch of her hand, so

soft, so gentle on his arm had him turning back to her.

"Cutter, do you know what the Amish people are known for?"

He was not really in the mood for a quiz. "No," he said with a resigned sigh. "But I have a feeling you're going to tell me."

"I am indeed going to tell you."

"Well, schoolmarm, I'm waiting."

"Compromise."

"Compromise?" he repeated, one eyebrow lifting. "What? Is this some kind of ethereal revelation I'm supposed to understand? What the hell does compromise have to do with you? With me? With what we feel for each other? And the worlds we come from?"

She merely kept smiling that serene smile. "It has everything to do with you and me and the worlds and families we come from," she said, taking a step closer to him. "You see things only in black and white, Cutter, while I see all the possibilities of compromise. It is our way."

He sighed, weary with fatigue, with wanting her, with trying to figure out a way they could be together. "Okay, I give up. What's the compromise?" He'd thought of every angle, every possibility, but still nothing made sense. There was no solution. He didn't want to admit the look on her face was starting to fill him with hope.

"Endy has accepted a position from your father as the caretaker of the Blackwell ranch."

"Okay," Cutter said with a sigh. "So Endy's going to stay on." He was surprised, but not overly so. Endy and Sadie had been scrabbling together from the moment they'd set eyes on each other. Any fool could see there was more there than either was willing to admit.

"I only teach nine months out of the year."

"I'm sure this makes some kind of sense somewhere, Sara, but I'll bite. So you only teach nine months of the year and Endy's staying here on the ranch. What of it?"

"The deacons and my family believe that your arrival was God's will."

"Okay," he said with a shrug, no longer as suspicious, the hope growing. "My arrival was God's will."

"My father said he would accept whatever happened because he would not be so bold as to defy or question God's will."

"Okay, so?"

She took a deep breath. "Okay. So what if we spent nine months of the year in Illinois so I could continue teaching. We could live in Endy's house since it will be empty and someone will need to care for it."

He let go of the tools he'd been holding in a death

grip, letting them drop unheeded to the ground. "Yeah, so, then what?"

"Well, for nine months I will teach at the settlement and still be able to see my family. My father, my mother and little Josef."

"Okay." He moved a step closer, the hope flaring brighter. "What about the other three months of the year."

"Well," she said pausing. "The other three months of the year, we could come back here, to Texas, so I—we—could spend time with Colt and the rest of your—our—family."

He wanted to be certain, absolutely certain, he understood what she was proposing. "So you're saying we'll live in both worlds?"

"In a manner of speaking. I, of course, will not live in the settlement nor will I live by the *Ordnung*. But I will still be able to teach in the settlement school and I will still be able to see my family and all of my friends."

"And so will I," he said, realizing the impact of what she was saying, almost afraid to believe it was possible. It *was* the best of both worlds. "But, Sara, would your people accept your marriage to an English man? What about the shunning thing?"

"I have not been baptized yet, so I cannot be shunned." She smiled at his concern. "Cutter, have you not been listening to me all this time? Everything that happens is God's will. We believe that family and faith are the most important things in the world. Our purpose for living. God brought you to me for a reason, and I believe that reason was more than just to reunite me with my natural brother.'' She cocked her head and smiled at him. ''God brought you to me because, Cutter Blackwell, you are my future. You are my family. Together we will make out own family. As God intended. One man. One woman.'' She glanced up at him shyly. ''That is, if you're willing to compromise.''

Stunned nearly speechless, he nodded his head. ''I can do that. I can definitely do that.'' He frowned. ''But what about you? You won't be living in the settlement. How will you feel about that?'' He never wanted her to regret this.

''No.'' She shook her head firmly. ''Cutter, if God did not want me to know who I really was, then you would never have found me. I know now that I am…English. I know now that the yearnings and desires deep in my heart were there so that when the time was right, I could accept your presence in my life.'' She laid her hand on his arm again. ''I understand that now. And if I truly believe as I have been taught, then I believe this is God's plan.'' She cocked her head to look at him. ''And so, will you, Cutter Blackwell, accept God's will, as well?''

He didn't have to think twice about it. He swung her up in his arms, saying a silent, fervent prayer of thanks. ''Absolutely, Sara Gunter. Absolutely.'' He kissed her long and hard. "Will you marry me, Sara Gunter?"

She wrapped her arms around him and held on tight. "Yes, Cutter Blackwell, I will marry you." She kissed him back. "I will make a life with you and a family with you, and we will share our lives with all of our families. As it should be. As it was intended."

Grinning, Cutter swung her higher, his heart finally, blissfully, at peace. "Sounds like a plan to me."

Chapter Thirteen

"Just follow me, Mrs. Blackwell," Endy said as he escorted Emma up the stairs toward the bedroom where Sara was dressing for her wedding. Emma and the whole family had been in Illinois for almost a week, getting everything ready for Sara and Cutter's wedding.

Endy knocked gently. "Sara, honey, there's someone here to see you." He opened the door, let Emma slip inside, then quietly shut it.

"Oh, Sara, honey." Emma's hand went to her mouth and tears filled her eyes. "You look... beautiful. Absolutely beautiful."

Sara felt her own tears well with happiness. Tenderly, she ran her hands down the beautiful while silk gown, intricately woven with beads and pearls. It was the most elegant thing she'd ever seen or worn. "Thank you," she said shyly, glancing down at the matching while silk bridal shoes Emma had purchased for her. "It was so wonderful of you to let me wear your wedding dress." She had to swallow the lump in her throat. "It is such...an honor to be given."

Emma went to her, taking her hands. "No, honey. It's my honor." She squeezed Sara's hands. "No bride has ever looked lovelier. I've never had a daughter, and it just seems fitting that you should wear my gown, and then, when your daughter gets married, I'd like you to pass it on to her."

"A new tradition?" Sara asked carefully, overwhelmed at the love and acceptance Cutter's family had extended to her.

"Yes," Emma said softly. "A new Blackwell family tradition." There was another knock at the door, and Emma released her hands. "Let me get it." Emma laughed. "It's probably my son. I don't think I've ever seen Cutter so nervous before." Emma's voice trailed off when she opened the door.

"May I come in?" Sara's mother stood hesitantly in the doorway, a large, plainly wrapped package under her arm.

"Mama." Sara went to her, drew her into the room and embraced her. In spite of all that had happened, she wanted to get married here, in Endy's garden, with her family surrounding her. It seemed only right to have both of her families joined on this day of joy. "Oh, Mama, please, do not cry."

"It's just…you look so…beautiful." Mary Gunter turned to Emma. "It was a kindness for you to give to my daughter such a beautiful dress."

Emma took the woman's hand. "No, it wasn't kindness, but love." Emma glanced at Sara. "I love Sara."

Beaming at her only daughter, Mary Gunter nodded. "Aye, she is an easy child to love." Nervously, Mary ran her hand over the package she was holding. "I…I have brought you something." She handed the package to Sara. "To begin your marriage. It is not fancy, but it—"

"Oh, Mama!" Sara's eyes welled with tears and reverently she unwrapped the gift, lifting her gaze to her mothers. "It is…it is my marriage quilt." Lovingly, Sara traced the intricate stitches of the quilt. She had once thought the traditions of her faith would be lost to her because of loving Cutter. But now, more than ever, she knew that she'd made the right decision. The only decision she could have made.

"Yes, daughter." Mary smiled, turning to Emma to explain. "It is…tradition. When a woman announces her intent to marry, all of the women of the *Gemeide* get together to sew her a marriage quilt. The mother of the bride takes a piece of quilt from her own marriage quilt to sew into her daughter's." She reached for a corner of the quilt Sara was still holding.

"This piece," she said softly. "It is from my own marriage quilt."

"How lovely," Emma said, gently touching the beautiful, exquisitely stitched fabric.

"It is said that the love of the mother and father are woven into each stitch so that the daughter and her new husband will always have an abundance of extra love in times of trouble." Mary touched her daughter's cheek, her eyes bright with tears. "I wish you much happiness and love, my daughter, on this, the day of your marriage." She patted Sara's cheek. "For all the days of your life." She took Sara's hand. "I love you, daughter, and I am proud of the woman you are."

"I love you, too, Mama," Sara said, her heart overflowing. "I love both of you," she added softly, her gaze going to Emma and then back to her mother.

"Uh, Mom?" Colt's voice filtered through the closed door. "How much longer till Sara's ready? Cutter's about to pace the grass into oblivion."

Laughing, Sara went to the door and opened it to her brother. "Colt, come in, please. There is someone for you to meet," she said. "Colt, this is my mother."

He extended his hand, and politely, Mary Gunter took it.

"Mama, this is my brother, Colt."

"Oh!" Mary's gaze flew to Colt's and she studied him for a moment, then her face broke into a wide smile. "It is so good to meet you, so good that Sara has found you." She continued to pump his hand. "I am so happy for both of you." She pressed a hand to her breast. "It was God's will," she whispered, saying a soft prayer. "A family, it should always be together." She patted his hand.

"I'm very happy to meet you," Colt said, covering Mary Gunter's hand with his own. "And thank you," he whispered in return, bending to kiss the older woman's cheek. "For taking such good care of my sister."

Smiling, Mary ducked her head to hide a blush.

"Uh, Mom." Colt glanced at Emma. "Can you guys get a move on? Cutter's making everyone crazy."

"We'll be right down."

Smiling, Sara handed Colt the marriage quilt. "Would you hold this for me and keep it safe until after the wedding?"

"Sure." Colt took the quilt and headed toward the door. "Just don't be too long," he warned over his shoulder as he headed back downstairs to calm his brother.

Sara and her mother exchanged glances and matching smiles.

"He is your son, then?" Mary asked Emma as Sara put her veil on.

"Yes. One of them."

Smiling, Mary nodded. "He will marry soon, then."

Emma laughed. "Colt?" She shook her head. "I doubt it. Colt claims he's not the marrying kind."

"Aye, so he says, but it is destined now." Mary flashed her a brilliant smile full of feminine wisdom.

"Why do you say that?" Emma asked curiously.

Again, Sara and her mother exchanged knowing glances.

"Emma," Sara explained, "it is said that whoever holds the marriage quilt, who honors it and keeps it safe, will be the next one to marry."

It was Emma's turn to look from one woman to the other. Then she grinned, a beautiful, ethereal grin. "You did that on purpose, didn't you, Sara?" Emma asked.

Sara nodded. "I hope that you don't mind."

"There is nothing more I could wish for Colt than to find a woman like you, Sara."

"Thank you." Sara patted her veil one last time. "And there is nothing more I could wish for my brother than to find the same happiness I have found."

Sara turned and glanced out the window. She could see Cutter pacing up and down in front of the makeshift canopy where they would recite their vows. The sight of him, so handsome in his dark suit, took her breath away.

"I am ready," she announced, letting out a slow breath and turning toward her mothers.

"Then it is time for you to start your new life," Mary said, reaching for one of her daughter's hands as well as Emma's. "And I cannot think of a better way to start your marriage than with your family around you. All of your family,'' she added, glancing shyly at Emma.

"Family is all that ever really matters," Emma said, earning a nod from Mary.

"And it is my joy to have both my families with me for this joyous day." Sara smiled. "Let us go, then, and join our families together."

They started toward the door, and Sara glanced back out the window and she smiled.

From this day forward, Cutter would be her husband, her family, and together they would make a life together, a life of happiness and love, a love that they would share with their children and grandchildren.

As it should be.

The ache of loneliness and uncertainty that she had lived with all of her life was finally gone.

Sara Gunter had finally found her family. She was…home.

* * * * *

*Be sure to look for the next book from
Sharon De Vita.
Don't miss Colt's story,
THE MARRIAGE BADGE,
on sale in April 2000.
Available in Silhouette Romance.*

THE FORTUNES OF TEXAS™

Membership in this family has its privileges…and its price. But what a fortune can't buy, a true-bred Texas love is sure to bring!

On sale in April…

Lone Star Wedding

by

SANDRA STEFFEN

Hannah Cassidy was planning the most memorable Fortune wedding ever. But she had to contend with Parker Malone, the Fortunes' handsome attorney. Although Parker swore he'd never say "I do," Hannah's deepest desire was to transform the commitment-wary loner into her Lone Star groom!

THE FORTUNES OF TEXAS continues with **IN THE ARMS OF A HERO** by Beverly Barton, on sale in May.

Available at your favorite retail outlet.

Where love comes alive™

Visit us at www.romance.net

PSFOT9

Look Who's celebrating Our 20th Anniversary:

Celebrate
20 YEARS

"Let's raise a glass to Silhouette and all the great books and talented authors they've introduced over the past twenty years. May the *next* twenty be just as exciting and just as innovative!"

—*New York Times* bestselling author
Linda Lael Miller

"A visit to Silhouette is a guaranteed happy ending, a chance to touch magic for a little while.... I hope Silhouette goes on forever."

—International bestselling author
Marie Ferrarella

"Twenty years of laughter and love. It's not hard to imagine Silhouette Books celebrating twenty years of quality publishing, but it is hard to imagine a publishing world without it. Congratulations."

—International bestselling author
Emilie Richards

Silhouette®SPECIAL EDITION®

Visit us at www.romance.net

PS20SSEAQ1

SILHOUETTE'S 20TH ANNIVERSARY CONTEST
OFFICIAL RULES
NO PURCHASE NECESSARY TO ENTER

1. To enter, follow directions published in the offer to which you are responding. Contest begins 1/1/00 and ends on 8/24/00 (the "Promotion Period"). Method of entry may vary. Mailed entries must be postmarked by 8/24/00, and received by 8/31/00.

2. During the Promotion Period, the Contest may be presented via the Internet. Entry via the Internet may be restricted to residents of certain geographic areas that are disclosed on the Web site. To enter via the Internet, if you are a resident of a geographic area in which Internet entry is permissible, follow the directions displayed on-line, including typing your essay of 100 words or fewer telling us "Where In The World Your Love Will Come Alive." On-line entries must be received by 11:59 p.m. Eastern Standard time on 8/24/00. Limit one e-mail entry per person, household and e-mail address per day, per presentation. If you are a resident of a geographic area in which entry via the Internet is permissible, you may, in lieu of submitting an entry on-line, enter by mail, by hand-printing your name, address, telephone number and contest number/name on an 8"x 11" plain piece of paper and telling us in 100 words or fewer "Where In The World Your Love Will Come Alive," and mailing via first-class mail to: Silhouette 20th Anniversary Contest, (in the U.S.) P.O. Box 9069, Buffalo, NY 14269-9069; (In Canada) P.O. Box 637, Fort Erie, Ontario, Canada L2A 5X3. Limit one 8"x 11" mailed entry per person, household and e-mail address per day. On-line and/or 8"x 11" mailed entries received from persons residing in geographic areas in which Internet entry is not permissible will be disqualified. No liability is assumed for lost, late, incomplete, inaccurate, nondelivered or misdirected mail, or misdirected e-mail, for technical, hardware or software failures of any kind, lost or unavailable network connection, or failed, incomplete, garbled or delayed computer transmission or any human error which may occur in the receipt or processing of the entries in the contest.

Essays will be judged by a panel of members of the Silhouette editorial and marketing staff based on the following criteria:

> Sincerity (believability, credibility)—50%
> Originality (freshness, creativity)—30%
> Aptness (appropriateness to contest ideas)—20%

Purchase or acceptance of a product offer does not improve your chances of winning. In the event of a tie, duplicate prizes will be awarded.

All entries become the property of Harlequin Enterprises Ltd., and will not be returned. Winner will be determined no later than 10/31/00 and will be notified by mail. Grand Prize winner will be required to sign and return Affidavit of Eligibility within 15 days of receipt of notification. Noncompliance within the time period may result in disqualification and an alternative winner may be selected. All municipal, provincial, federal, state and local laws and regulations apply. Contest open only to residents of the U.S. and Canada who are 18 years of age or older, and is void wherever prohibited by law. Internet entry is restricted solely to residents of those geographical areas in which Internet entry is permissible. Employees of Torstar Corp., their affiliates, agents and members of their immediate families are not eligible. Taxes on the prizes are the sole responsibility of winners. Entry and acceptance of any prize offered constitutes permission to use winner's name, photograph or other likeness for the purposes of advertising, trade and promotion on behalf of Torstar Corp. without further compensation to the winner, unless prohibited by law. Torstar Corp and D.L. Blair, Inc., their parents, affiliates and subsidiaries, are not responsible for errors in printing or electronic presentation of contest or entries. In the event of printing or other errors which may result in unintended prize values or duplication of prizes, all affected contest materials or entries shall be null and void. If for any reason the Internet portion of the contest is not capable of running as planned, including infection by computer virus, bugs, tampering, unauthorized intervention, fraud, technical failures, or any other causes beyond the control of Torstar Corp. which corrupt or affect the administration, secrecy, fairness, integrity or proper conduct of the contest, Torstar Corp. reserves the right, at its sole discretion, to disqualify any individual who tampers with the entry process and to cancel, terminate, modify or suspend the contest or the Internet portion thereof. In the event of a dispute regarding an on-line entry, the entry will be deemed submitted by the authorized holder of the e-mail account submitted at the time of entry. Authorized account holder is defined as the natural person who is assigned to an e-mail address by an Internet access provider, on-line service provider or other organization that is responsible for arranging e-mail address for the domain associated with the submitted e-mail address.

Prizes: Grand Prize—a $10,000 vacation to anywhere in the world. Travelers (at least one must be 18 years of age or older) or parent or guardian if one traveler is a minor, must sign and return a Release of Liability prior to departure. Travel must be completed by December 31, 2001, and is subject to space and accommodations availability. Two hundred (200) Second Prizes—a two-book limited edition autographed collector set from one of the Silhouette Anniversary authors: Nora Roberts, Diana Palmer, Linda Howard or Annette Broadrick (value $10.00 each set). All prizes are valued in U.S. dollars.

For a list of winners (available after 10/31/00), send a self-addressed, stamped envelope to: Harlequin Silhouette 20th Anniversary Winners, P.O. Box 4200, Blair, NE 68009-4200.

Contest sponsored by Torstar Corp., P.O. Box 9042, Buffalo, NY 14269-9042.

PS20RULES

ENTER FOR A CHANCE TO WIN*

Silhouette's 20th Anniversary Contest

Tell Us Where in the World You Would Like *Your* Love To Come Alive... And We'll Send the Lucky Winner There!

Silhouette wants to take you wherever your happy ending can come true.

Here's how to enter: Tell us, in 100 words or less, where you want to go to make your love come alive!

In addition to the grand prize, there will be 200 runner-up prizes, collector's-edition book sets autographed by one of the Silhouette anniversary authors: **Nora Roberts, Diana Palmer, Linda Howard** or **Annette Broadrick**.

DON'T MISS YOUR CHANCE TO WIN! ENTER NOW! No Purchase Necessary

Silhouette®
Where love comes alive™

Name: _____

Address: _____

City: _____ State/Province: _____

Zip/Postal Code: _____

Mail to Harlequin Books: **In the U.S.:** P.O. Box 9069, Buffalo, NY 14269-9069; **In Canada:** P.O. Box 637, Fort Erie, Ontario, L4A 5X3

*No purchase necessary—for contest details send a self-addressed stamped envelope to Silhouette's 20th Anniversary Contest, P.O. Box 9069, Buffalo, NY, 14269-9069 (includ contest name on self-addressed envelope). Residents of Washington and Vermont ma omit postage. Open to Cdn. (excluding Quebec) and U.S. residents who are 18 or ove Void where prohibited. Contest ends August 31, 2000.

PS20CON_